BLACK BOTTLE MAN

BLACK BOTTLE MAN

CRAIG RUSSELL

Great Plains Teen Fiction
(an imprint of Great Plains Publications)
1173 Wolseley Avenue
Winnipeg, MB R3G 1H1
www.greatplains.mb.ca

Great Plains Publications gratefully acknowledges the financial support
provided for its publishing program by the Government of Canada
through the Canada Book Fund; the Canada Council for the Arts;
the Province of Manitoba through the Book Publishing Tax Credit
and the Book Publisher Marketing Assistance Program; and the
Manitoba Arts Council.

Design & Typography by Relish New Brand Experience

Printed in Canada by Friesens
Fourth printing, 2020

Library and Archives Canada Cataloguing in Publication

Russell, Craig, 1956 June 18-
Black bottle man / Craig Russell.

ISBN 978-1-894283-99-1

I. Title.

PS8635.U868B53 2010   jC813'.6   C2009-906684-X

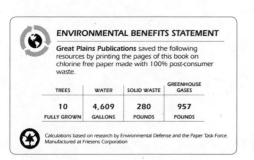

A fable for my mother and father.
A story of true love for my wife.
An adventure for my son and daughter.

1 Rembrandt — 2007

IN FIVE MINUTES Rembrandt celebrates his ninetieth birthday. Then he has thirty days to live.

Not that anyone here will be baking him a cake. It's his first night at this shelter, but the Salvation Army folk are always good to him wherever he goes. Always good for a hot meal and a warm cot, but they have plenty on their plates already.

This Sally Anne dormitory stinks, but Rembrandt is used to the reek of unwashed bodies. In homeless shelters across Canada and the U.S. he has inhaled the musk of men who stumble through life, the sour odour of women too shattered to care. And before there were such things as homeless shelters, he'd shared countless shanties with hobos and migrant workers from Texas to Alaska.

For eighty long years, Rembrandt has been on the move. But he is not like the others in this cot-filled hall. He's not a drunk, nor an addict, nor currently, a mad-man. Nevertheless, he moves on every twelve days. Sometimes sooner if a place offers too much of its own trouble. But he never stays longer than the twelve.

Like an Eleventh Commandment, "The Pact" has fixed that unrelenting time limit. It is part of a bargain that has ruled and ruined his family for four score years, a covenant forged from family pride and maternal desire. As unforgiving as an iron rod laid upon his shoulders, a burden at first shared with his pa and Uncle Thompson, but now carried onward by him alone.

Back in '32, when Rembrandt was a boy, his Uncle Thompson had broken that rule, staying in one place longer than the requisite twelve days.

They'd meant to pass through Billings, Montana but Thompson got himself hired on to break horses, while young Rembrandt, at fifteen, was handed a pitchfork and told to muck out the barn.

The horses were beauts. Wild mustangs trapped by the ranchers, and everyone said Thompson was a dab hand at breaking them. Making good money at two dollars for a mare and five for a cut stallion, they put away ten dollars a day or more. Far better than the dollar-a-day strong-back jobs they usually found. With that kind of folding money, plans were made to buy some badly needed boots.

Maybe the Devil got into that horse. Or maybe a ranch-hand wanted to take Thompson down a notch. As the boy was to learn, in life often the *why* doesn't matter so much as the *what*. And the *what* that day was him at age fifteen driving an unsprung wagon down a long, hard-rut road, with the man who'd stood in for his pa for the last four years lying in the back, near broke in half by pride and a wild horse.

But that wasn't the worst of it. The twelve day deadline was coming.

Soon Thompson was in the hospital, encased in plaster and high on morphine, when what he needed most was to be moved to another town. Rembrandt offered all the money they had to make it happen, but the doctor just took it to pay the bill and left them with empty pockets. Who listens to a fifteen-year-old boy, either then or now?

On day twelve Thompson had been just fine, barring a broken hip that was already healing and a head too doped up to think of escape.

Young Rembrandt wanted to drag him out of there, but instead he let the injured man dissuade him.

"You go down to the switching yard," Thompson said. "Find a freight headed to Missoula. I'll catch up in a few days."

Lying in that hospital bed, trapped like an amber fly, Thompson swore he wouldn't talk to any preachers. "And with all we've learned to do with the signs, I'll be fine."

For himself, Rembrandt had no worries. He was big for his age and thought he could scrap pretty good. Before he left though, his uncle made him recite all the hobo signs and checked their bindles, transferring a few things from his own into the boy's cloth sack.

Word of bad things has a way to travel like good news can't.

Two days later in Missoula, Rembrandt was there when a drunken hobo told the whole camp about how, "Three folks down in the Billings hospital had died. Died real bad."

He knew his numbers. It had been on day thirteen.

Since then Rembrandt's been on his own.

Uncle Thompson had been a good man. Almost like having Pa around. God he missed Pa, even after eighty years.

They'd been close, Uncle Thompson and Pa. Close with their sister Annie too. She was the middle one of the three.

They were tight like families used to be, always talking and helping out with the chores.

Their farms were each built in the closest corner of their homestead quarters, making a crossroads of sorts, with the fourth corner empty, save for a hay meadow.

Not many homesteaders built that way. Most came west as single families, bent on making their own way in the world. So all other things being equal, those families built in the middle of their hundred-and-sixty acre land grants. It made sense for a single family. Your fields would all be closer that way and you'd waste less time hiking about to seed, or weed, or harvest.

Building the three houses close together like that was unusual enough that people thereabouts took to calling it "Three Farms."

Annie's husband, Rembrandt's Uncle Billy, his pa and Uncle Thompson were all hard working men, not afraid of honest sweat. Together, the three men and their wives broke that land, folding virgin prairie into furrows so rich, black and alive you knew what Eden must have felt like before The Fall. And together they built the three homes, including the one where Rembrandt was born in 1917.

Sometimes the night smells in a Sally Ann hall took Old Rembrandt back to Three Farms.

He'd held a special place in those homes.

Uncle Billy said, "The only child among three couples, he's as welcome as rain on a dusty day."

Uncle Thompson's wife, his Aunt Emma helped with his birthing and told his ma, "I want six just like him."

But by the time young Rembrandt turned ten no other babies had come. You could see how it took the wind out of his aunts Annie and Emma.

"All that hard work."

"Every day, for years."

"And for what?"

Young women nowadays have choices their great-grammas could never have imagined. Reproductive choice, it's called. But even at ten Rembrandt had known what choice those two women would've made.

"We want babies."

"Even just one."

"Please."

Aunt Annie started writing their folks back east, hinting about how things were. Soon it was a letter every month, after her blood flowed, regular as a clock. She and her two brothers had kin in Quebec who were doctors and Annie asked for any medicine they might send to help with "the problem."

"It's a waste of good money." Uncle Billy said. "All those postage stamps. All that paper."

But Annie was one to have her own way and "Billy-be-damned" as the saying goes.

The adults were all too busy with chores to make an extra trip into town, so Aunt Annie entrusted her messages to young Rembrandt.

People today can hardly credit how much time it took back then just to keep body and soul together: split wood to feed the stove, to heat the water, to make the porridge, just to have breakfast. More pure physical effort went into making that bowl of cereal than most folks now expend in a full day at the office.

Truth be told, it made Rembrandt feel important, tucking Annie's letters into his shirt, wrapped in waxed paper as safeguard against bad weather or the mishaps a spirited boy might find. He didn't mind helping out and carrying an envelope that would travel so far away felt like a piece of adventure was pressed against his chest.

Like everything else in town, the post office was new. Built of Tyndall stone and brick, it smelled of ink and importance. The two men who worked there, the postmaster and the clerk, wore tightly knotted neckties and stiff white shirts, as faithful to their oath, borrowed from the couriers of ancient Babylon, as any doctor to Hippocrates, and the boy was eyed for any hint of mischief.

Rembrandt never spoke aloud in that temple to the written word, and the two men worked in hushed murmurs that suited the gravity of a task that had not yet been made cheap and vulgar by junk mail and grocery-store flyers.

It was 1927, the summer Rembrandt turned ten, when the postmaster's pronouncement — "Package from Montreal for your Aunt Annie." — transformed the boy into a messenger from Marathon, hurdling out the front door with news too important to wait on dignity or convention.

Legs and arms suffused with a sympathetic energy come at last to term, he flew along the dirt track road for home, for Aunt Annie's hope. Still a good mile from Three Farms he started shouting.

"Package!" Unable to contain the word. A dozen sprinting strides, two bellows breaths and the shout became his cadence. "Package! — Package!"

The open prairie swallows the human voice whole, but a mother's ear is tuned to her child's cry, so for the last flat half-mile a figure that could only be his ma was at the end of the lane, watching him run. She was soon joined by the other adults.

"Package!" he shouted again. As repeated words will, it had become abstracted and strange in his mouth. Then he heard a voice, high-pitched and feminine, excited and feverish, echoing the word back to him.

"Package!" It was Aunt Annie. She understood the import, the promise of his call.

Under her impatient gaze Uncle Billy had the team and wagon ready lickety-split and then he and Rembrandt retraced the path to town. The boy sat beside Annie's husband like a conquering Caesar, ready to claim the postman's prize.

When they finally unloaded the wooden box from Montreal, with "Fragile — Glass" stencilled on the outside, Emma and Annie were beside themselves.

"Careful."

"Careful!"

More than once since then Rembrandt has wished he'd been a lot more clumsy that day.

His uncles carried the treasure inside Thompson and Emma's house, and the three couples crowded into their kitchen to open the box. Young Rembrandt was excluded. It was adult business and little boys could fend for themselves.

Months later, when they were on the move, Uncle Thompson told him some of what happened. Some things he guessed at. Some he found out later when he went to Montreal.

The box held two things — a glass bottle and a letter. Separate they would have been curiosities, like in the Ripley's *Believe It or Not* show. Together they were the end of Rembrandt's young world.

The letter was from "a friend of a friend of a cousin." Someone who'd heard about "those poor women out west who want babies so bad."

The writer said he'd been to Black Africa and seen things that the missionaries were busy suppressing.

Black magic, he said. He didn't want to fool them. That's what this was — *black magic*.

They could use it, or they could throw it away. That was up to them. You couldn't force black magic on someone who didn't want it. It was their choice, he said.

The letter had diagrams and pictures, things they were supposed to draw on their bodies — both men and women— using ink from the bottle. There were circles and lines that weren't quite right, like those trick pictures in puzzle books where three rods look like they should be four instead.

It was all laid out, step by step, like an old-time dance-lesson diagram. Steps for the woman, and steps for her partner.

The bottle was black. Not like it was made black, but like the black was coming out from what was inside, changing the glass just by how mean it was.

It had a stopper of yellow ivory, the colour of a tobacco-chewer's back teeth, carved to look like a sad little man, praying for something that wouldn't do him any good even if he got it.

The men were against it of course. No way in Hell would they truck with the Devil.

Thompson said, "We know our place in God's world and it's at the feet of Jesus Lord."

"I'll smash the damned bottle," Uncle Billy swore. He and Rembrandt's pa had moved some big rocks up from the creek on the stone-boat earlier that day, getting ready to lay a new barn foundation. "That'll do the trick."

But before Billy could turn words into action, Aunt Annie snatched up the letter and the bottle both, and ran out of the house.

Rembrandt saw that part of things, though he didn't understand it at the time. Hanging upside-down in the big elm that shaded Emma's back porch, he was enjoying the simple juvenile thrill of letting all the blood rush to his head, when Annie cannoned out of Emma's kitchen door and handed him their future.

"Quick. Hide these." She whispered as though it were a game, like hide-and-seek. Then she ran, headed for the out-buildings.

Rembrandt curled back right-side up, the black bottle in one small hand, the folded paper in the other and disappeared from sight into the dappling green. The tree's canopy darkened, he thought from the upside-down blood draining from his brain, and his hands tingled hard with pins and needles.

"Annie!" Uncle Billy roared past a few feet below him and his fleeing Aunt ducked behind a shed, playing decoy, like a mother killdeer leading the fox away from her shallow gravel nest.

Rembrandt tucked the paper into the tree-crotch where its branch clove to the main trunk and jammed the bottle in tight after it, holding both fast. He didn't want to let Aunt Annie down and felt sure no one could see her treasures from the ground.

Billy unbuckled his belt, aiming to make his wife tell where she'd hidden the contraband, but Pa and Uncle Thompson loved their sister too much to let him. Billy was some mad but the three men eventually agreed that so long as he and Thompson didn't let their wives paint them up, the black magic would be useless.

Later, Uncle Thompson said that Rembrandt's ma had been quiet through the whole thing. He reckoned that she agreed with the men, but couldn't come right out and say so in front of her sisters-in-law. In those days, keeping the family peace was a big part of being a wife and mother.

Plus they lived a long way from any neighbours and you'd do a lot to keep your only friends from hating you. Because that was what Ma must have thought — that they might hate her — over her having a son and them having none, nor a daughter either.

Rembrandt thought that maybe if he'd never been born, Emma and Annie might not have been so sad, and they might not have done the Devil's work.

TIME HEALS ALL WOUNDS.

That's what Gail's mother told her, back when she was a girl. Except, it doesn't.

Here in her stairwell nest only her precious metronome can keep the wounds at bay. Wind it up and snatch sleep for fifteen minutes while it tick — tick — ticks. Knowing that when it stops, the dream of spinning brass will come.

Hear the whip-crack of passing death and startle awake like the electro-shock therapy they'd promised would cure her. Rewind with shaking hands and clutch at sleep again while the metronome takes time's measure. Add another layer of sweating panic when it stops. Over and over again — until morning comes and she can go back to watching the school.

She pulls off a mismatched glove and in the faint glimmer of her wedding band recalls Raymond. He tried to cope. First separate beds, then separate bedrooms. Counsellors who talked and therapists who listened, forty-five minutes each session, then gone, onto the next case.

And doctors, and doctors, and *doctors*, who diagnosed and drugged her, until she said "Enough!" and made the choice she knew Raymond could not. As much as he loved her, he could not save her.

She hopes that by leaving, she has given him a chance of salvaging a life for himself.

Her route to the school will be safe so long as she follows the "glass rule." The glass rule is simple — always pick up any broken glass you see.

Broken glass is dangerous. People who break glass...well, you try not to think about them.

Today starts off easy. A single broken bottle means she gets to the school in plenty of time to watch the buses unload. That's always a good thing. Seeing the kids running in the front door lets her breathe for a whole hour without having to think about the spinning brass. And that makes it easier to follow the "3-5-9 rule."

Once you're at the school, you just have to say —"Three-five-nine" — exactly right, exactly a hundred times, and then nothing bad can happen for the rest of that day. If you say it just right, then 3-5-9 can't come back and break the glass and no one will die.

Gail is very careful with 3-5-9.

She has her fingers and those make it easy to do sets of ten. Marking each ten completed on the sidewalk with a piece of yellow chalk stolen from her old classroom makes it child's play. So long as no one interrupts her count, the task will be completed and for one more day the children will be safe.

But while she counts, she looks around, scouting for interfering busybodies.

Parents drive up to drop their kids off and no one bothers her. Except... There are two women talking and pointing at her. One, the mother of a former pupil, is coming over. The stupid woman is going to talk to Gail during 3-5-9!

She tries so hard not to be distracted, but the woman is all big and caring and — and Gail loses count. She loses track of 3-5-9. Starting over will do no good. That might make it worse.

There isn't any other choice. Someone has to pay.

Reaching into her coat-pocket Gail's hand closes around a piece of that morning's broken glass. She hadn't noticed before, but it's a pretty thing in its own way, a brown and scalloped triangle, like a flint arrowhead; a random work of art in her random, artless life. A quick, raking stab sinks it into Gail's dirty forearm, and her blood flows.

That's good. When 3-5-9 comes he'll have to take her to the hospital, and the children will be okay.

As Gail knew she would, the caring mum calls 911 and a police car comes. Badge Number 3-5-9 doesn't get out. Some other policeman does. 3-5-9 must be the other one, the one still sitting in the car.

She starts to feel dizzy, but as she faints she knows it will be okay. She's paid the price and the children will be safe for today.

3 Rembrandt — 2007

EARLY MORNING AT ANY SALLY ANN is a good time to be invisible.

Old Rembrandt knows this from long experience. Come morning the drunks are hung over and the druggies are already looking to score their first fix. Miserable people and desperate people make a bad combination. Throw in an over-enthusiastic Salvation Army volunteer and you've got a recipe for trouble.

Staying invisible when no one is looking for you is pretty easy. Nothing to it, really. Even your own spit will work for a little while with that kind of Simple Simon magic. But you need something strong to make a sign on your skin that will last.

This morning he's lucky. The Army folk are old hands. They have plenty of coffee ready before anyone is up, extra strong. Even a drunk or an addict can get a little buzz off a strong cup of joe — at least enough to get them out the door with a day-old bagel in their hand, off to face another day of begging, or stealing, or worse.

The Army people don't know it, but their coffee is even strong enough to use for "skin-signs." Least ways for an hour or two until it gets stale. A cup of Sally Ann coffee, well, it's like the holy sacrament — with caffeine added.

When the worst of the pain-filled people have stumbled out of the hall, Rembrandt lets the *don't see me* go, and speaks to each of the Army staff. They deserve to be thanked for what they put up with, and he was raised to respect folks who do for others.

He puts out his hand and they each take it. The chance to shake their hands is a blessing for him too. In eleven days he'll have moved on and there isn't much human touch left in the world of a ninety-year-old man.

And there's always a chance that he might find a champion.

He's been looking most of his life to find a champion, and even though The Pact will run out soon, he's not ready to give up quite yet. "Ninety years plus thirty days" had been the deal and he'll take every last hour he's got.

Why Pa insisted on the extra thirty days had puzzled the Black Bottle Man. Four-score-and-ten would have been standard, but Pa had always been a hard bargainer, and so he'd refused to sign without the extra thirty days.

"Besides," Pa had said, "puzzling the Devil is its own reward."

Time was when Aunt Annie had been a fresh young beauty.

Old Rembrandt knew that that is true for all young women, if they only had the eyes of an old man to see it. But young Rembrandt, being a boy, could never see his aunt quite the way that Uncle Billy had, with a heart that erased lines and fading hair, with years of love and devotion.

"To me," Billy said, "my Annie is an angel."

So when the wooden box from Montreal came and caused all the trouble, Uncle Billy was like a ship that had lost its anchor.

"How could my angel," he asked, "the woman who saved me from demon rum and brought me back to Jesus, even think about what that letter suggests?"

Between the two of them there were hard words, and there's few on Earth as can cut a man deeper than his childless wife.

For Billy it was a dark time and he fell back into drinking. You couldn't hide such a thing of course, not with Prohibition on, the three farms being so close, and people spending half their days together. Not that he tried to keep it a secret.

Pa and Uncle Thompson looked at Billy pretty sharp, but he just told them, "Mind your own damn business."

And being who they were, that was a pretty sophisticated argument. It's not that they were simple. None of the adults were. They'd just been raised with a stiff-backed independence-of-mind drilled into them.

"You either find your way to Jesus," Pa said, "or you don't. If you don't, well, that's why God gave mankind free will. John Stuart Mill be praised."

So Uncle Billy got stewed, but good. And his wife, the angel Annie, did nothing to stop him.

Why Ma or Pa or Uncle Thompson didn't see what that would lead to, Rembrandt didn't know. Maybe the brothers could only see the good in their sister. Maybe Ma couldn't say anything bad to Pa about Annie.

However it was, nice, sweet Aunt Annie who took the instruction letter and the black bottle — kept hidden for her by a ten-year-old boy — and one moonless summer night she saw to it that her husband was stewed, tattooed and screwed.

4 The Elm —— 1927

"WAKE UP."

Without moonlight Rembrandt's square little room was dark as ink. His down pillow and comforter had been scattered by unwelcome dreams. He stood, quartered by window mullions and found a shape outside in the starlight. His Aunt Annie.

She signed her desire for secrecy, finger to lips, and pantomimed his progress through the house and outside to join her.

The rhythm of his parents' sleep was a quiet background to the summer evening's chorus. Frogs, silent through the hunting-hawk day had found their croaking voices. Crickets rubbed legs and made a sound all out of proportion to their size.

Barefoot in dew-wet grass he found her, with matching bare feet, in a flannel nightgown. He'd never seen his aunt in her bed-clothes before and a sudden awkwardness fell on him.

Across the road in the south house, Annie's and Billy's home, a coal oil lantern burned, throwing a watery light out their second-storey bedroom window like a piece of Alexandria's lost beacon calling sailors home from the sea.

Annie looked toward her house and the outline of a man staggered across the light, a liquor bottle held to his lips.

"The letter," she said. "I want it. And the black bottle."

Her face presented Rembrandt with a smile that held something fierce in check. A look that said: "Do as I say, please, and *now*."

They crossed the dirt road east to Thompson and Emma's yard, treading silty-sand wagon ruts, cooler still than the grass. The dew on their feet became a film of mud that coated their soles.

The elm tree outside Emma's kitchen was a black mass twitching in the lightest of winds. The sound held a wooden pain like quiet splinters.

Rembrandt had not climbed Emma's elm since the day Aunt Annie played the hiding game and made him take the two treasures. There'd been no reason to avoid climbing that tree, but he would've found a dozen excuses not to, if asked.

He stopped just outside the elm's canopy, this side of the faint ring formed by rain drops that marked its boundary, and pointed to the tree-crotch that held Annie's secrets, hoping she would retrieve them herself.

But she took his elbow and pulled him into the deeper shadow. She pushed him on and more by feel than sight he found the trunk. His fingers and toes pinched into crevices in the bark that felt like mouths, ready to bite.

"Up," she hissed, and he lunged upward, the top of his shoulder finding his hanging-branch.

"Oow!"

It didn't really hurt, but he leapt at the excuse to make a sound. Perhaps Emma or Thompson would hear them and save him from this changeling aunt.

"Quiet."

"Sorry."

"Quiet!"

"Okay."

"Shut—"

They both fell silent. Emma's kitchen door opened and another night-gowned woman appeared.

But Emma did not call out. No "Who's there?" let Rembrandt speak again. Instead, Emma stepped down from the porch, into the deeper shadow, a third in the barefoot night.

"Go away," said Annie.

"No." Emma's reply was quiet but held ready a petulant hint that she might call the others if she didn't get her way. "I want it too."

"Billy's drunk. Thompson isn't."

"Oh." That stopped Emma, but did not send her back inside.

"Rembrandt. Hand down the secrets. Carefully." Annie was back on track.

The hollow where he'd put the letter and the black bottle felt different now: bigger, deeper, like the elm tree had drawn back from the hidden items, trying not to touch them. No longer shallow, he had to reach further and further into the elm's heartwood, past bark and sap-sticky new growth, now smelling a rot inside the tree that had no right to be there.

If not for Annie's hisses he would never have done this, but he knew there'd be no coming down empty-handed.

His fingertips found something. Not the smooth curve of glass, but something carved and grooved. He knew it. The stopper. The image of the little ivory man bent in prayer.

It was what he was after, but Rembrandt feared to pull at it. Would the stopper hold? Would the bottle slide off, toppling, spilling the ink? Ruining the letter?

"Gentle, gentle." He couldn't help whispering aloud, twisting his grip, willing the neck up to where he might grab the bottle itself. The tingling was back in his hand, the circulation cut off at the shoulder by rough bark. Then it came, not free, but up and out, like a jack-in-the-box that had just been waiting to be sprung.

The letter was there too, stuck to the bottom of the bottle by a bit of sap, whole and intact.

"Here."

He handed the items down, anxious to be back in his bed.

By the time he'd clambered down, Annie was already on the move, Emma following, both headed straight for Annie and Billy's house.

Neither aunt spoke, but in the space of a hundred steps they'd invented a sign language that conveyed their every sentiment. Young Rembrandt, not privy to the subtleties of the adult world, thought he had the gist of things and worried that if he understood things right then some poor animal was apt to be slaughtered by these two women.

Trailing a long third, more aiming to the middle path between his parents' home and the south house, he was hurt and confused by how completely Aunt Annie had abandoned him.

From the road, he saw the two women disappear through the front doorway into Annie and Billy's home and then some trick of the lantern light threw too many shadows in Annie and Billy's second floor bedroom. Where there should only be two, a third joined in.

Hoping home and bed could quell this disquiet Rembrandt stole through Ma and Pa's house, back to his room.

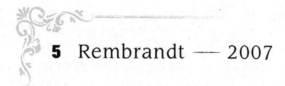

5 Rembrandt — 2007

BEFORE TAKING LEAVE of the Sally Ann hall, Old Rembrandt makes time to wash and have a shave. The face that looks back from the mirror is tight over angular cheeks and brow. Thin from years of missed meals and hard work. And his ears look like the Fuller Brush man has made a big sale.

The shave is quick. The whiskers on his chin seem to be taking lessons from the sparse hair on his head. Both are thin and tardy pupils. It won't take the Lord long to count the hairs on *his* head today.

A wash is always good, with soap and hot water to clear away the remnants of yesterday's skin-signs. It's nice to have a clean canvas in case luck, good or bad, comes to visit today.

6 Rembrandt — 1928

IT WAS UNCLE THOMPSON who made the first connection about the signs.

Living on the road meant learning the hobo life. Hobos had their own little society with rules and particular ways of seeing things. And their own form of communication.

It was called "hobo sign." And it was worth the trouble to learn.

Say a hobo found a good spot to lie up if he was hurt, or a place to avoid because the folks there liked to sic their dogs on strangers. He'd share that news by carving a mark in a hidden place nearby, where most folks would never think to look. It might be on the underside of a fence rail or the under-hang of a rock.

The signs were too vague for normal people to understand.

A double diamond told you that this was "*a good place to keep quiet.*"

A triangle with stick hands meant "*a man with a gun lives here.*"

When they first set out, Pa and Thompson didn't know anything about the hobo signs. But it didn't take long before they saw that there was a deeper knowledge to being on the road than the two brothers had between them.

So, sitting with some old hands in a Minnesota camp, near where the source of the Red River came close to kissing the tail of the Mississippi, Uncle Thompson let on that he was, "Trying to teach my nephew here, young Rembrandt, his hobo signs," and, "Would you fine gentlemen be willing to help?"

This was back before the Dirty Thirties, when it was just the men with a soul to travel who were out on the road. When the Great Depression came, things were different.

Many of the Depression hobos were men from good families. Men more like Pa and Thompson. Men who'd had farms and businesses, and who would never have left hearth and home, if it hadn't been for drought and grasshoppers and politicians with hearts of stone.

Some folks thought hobos were invented by the Great Depression. But that was wrong.

Rembrandt came to learn their history, how there had been hobo camps from the moment the first railway built a line between one city and the next.

"For some men," Pa said, "Wanderlust is a sickness that the railways carry from town to town like the smallpox. Show them a train and without a spot of a lesson they'll see a way to ride the rails."

Of course, he, Rembrandt and Uncle Thompson were on the road long before the Great Depression came.

So Uncle Thompson asked. And the hobo gentlemen were happy to help. It was a subject they warmed to and once young Rembrandt had pricked his thumb and been sworn into the secret brotherhood, the lessons began. He was an eager pupil and the men could see that he applied himself to the job. No whiner, he.

So the willow switch they'd cut to help with the lessons was used to draw the signs in the dirt and not once was it laid across his britches. Rembrandt wanted to make his pa proud and he could see that the hobo gentlemen gave the father a higher regard because the son was worth talking to.

The gentlemen didn't mind that Pa and Thompson stayed to watch and learn as well.

Old Rembrandt thought the men had been sharp enough to see the truth of things, but they chose to let Pa and Uncle Thompson keep a scrap of their pride intact.

It might not seem like much of a fall from grace to folks today, giving up a dry-land dirt farm and taking piecework from farmers and ranchers along the railroad. But Rembrandt saw how it cut Pa and Uncle Thompson across the grain.

Before the Black Bottle Man came, they'd been their own masters. Saving for God and the weather, their fate was their own. Now they were dollar-a-day field-hands — if they could get that good a job. If not, it might be ten hours splitting wood, just for meals and a dry hayloft to sleep in.

❊

When Uncle Thompson made his discovery, you'd have thought he'd swallowed a lightning bug. He was like the man Rembrandt remembered, from before The Pact was signed.

Thompson ran up fast as a tornado wind, hopping and whirling around, too excited to stand still. He had a secret that he was busting to share with them and they had to, "Come see, right now!"

They followed him out of the camp into a little wood split by a stream, where he'd been fishing for their supper. There on the grass bank, next to the stream, all lined up with a willow branch threaded through their gills, were five of the biggest, fattest trout-fish either Pa or Rembrandt had ever seen.

Pa was impressed and he said so. Rembrandt was hungry for a fish fry and he said so.

"But you don't see," said Thompson. He pointed at a log next to the stream. There, carved into the wood, was the hobo sign for *good fishin'*.

"So?" Pa said, "You can read the signs. Go to the front of the class."

"No," Thompson said. "The sign wasn't here when I found the place. I made the sign. And not *after* the fish were caught. It's not a sign to tell others that I found good fishin' here.

"I'd been sitting, hoping for a bite for over an hour. But with not a nibble, out of boredom I cut the sign into the log for practice.

"When I finished, I spat on it and rubbed it to make the grain stand out — and Wham! I had a bite. And she was a beaut! Then as fast as I could worm the hook, four more were flopping on the bank. Don't you see? My hobo sign *made* the fish come. It made this spot a place for good fishin'."

Pa looked at his brother, his face all tight and wrinkled, like when he'd dickered with the Black Bottle Man.

But Uncle Thompson swore with hand-on-heart, "I'm a God-fearing man, pledged still to Jesus Lord, Saviour above."

Pa had to take him at his word and the three of them set to puzzling it out.

⋛⋚

The five big trout were a seven-day wonder back at the camp. The hobo gentlemen were pleased to share in — "the bounty which we are about to receive" — though Rembrandt was sure he could eat a whole one himself.

He thought there was no way five trout could give everyone in the camp a fish-feed. But it must have been like the miracle of the loaves and the fishes. Because when that meal was done every man there was full, feeling fat and happy.

Pa sat a long while thinking on the mysterious ways, reflecting on how once, one man fed a multitude, and he had a change of heart on what Uncle Thompson had done.

"Maybe the Lord means to give us a hand at beating the Black Bottle Man," Pa said. "We could sure use the help."

Of course, Uncle Thompson had to show all the hobo gentlemen the fishing hole where he'd made the big catch. He didn't point out that he'd made a good fishin' sign to show others the right spot. After all, that was just expected.

But in the few days they remained in that camp, no one else, not even Pa or Rembrandt could catch another trout there. No worm, no fly, no secret spoon would snag even a small fry. Nor up nor down a good stretch of that whole stream.

"You're a damned liar," one of the hobos said, "Making the good fishin' sign there."

"He must be keepin' the real fishin' hole a secret for hisself," the man announced to the camp.

From the flat-iron look on Thompson's face Rembrandt thought it might come to blows. But at Pa's suggestion, with witnesses watching, Uncle Thompson threw in a line, and in two seconds flat pulled out one more beaut.

Everyone agreed, it was Thompson's fishing hole and that was that. Then the three of them had to move on and leave it behind, so it wasn't his for long either.

7 Rembrandt — 2007

SLEEPING AT A SALLY ANN is about as close as Rembrandt ever gets to a church these days. Ministers and priests just never take a shine to the old man. They aren't specifically rude to him, but somehow when he's around, their sermons take on a serious hellfire and damnation tone.

A piece back, when he needed to remind himself that he was still alive, he'd gone to services, just to see the surprised looks on the parishioners' faces when a stuffy old priest or newly ordained minister lit into the congregation about "The wages of sin and the whore of Babylon!"

Hearing the comments outside afterwards made it worth the scorched ears.

"Great sermon Reverend!" Folks would say, meaning: "Jesus, were you talking about me?"

Once, as a kind of experiment, he went to every service held in a failing Catholic Church for twelve days straight, and saw the attendance jump from five old ladies on the first day to two hundred souls on the last.

Seems there's some that just want to be told they've been bad. Makes them feel like someone's paying attention.

It was a good thing he'd had to move on, or the strain might have sent that poor old priest on to his own reward.

8 Rembrandt — 1928

TRAVELLING WITH PA AND UNCLE THOMPSON was something young Rembrandt too soon took for granted. It wasn't until later that he saw how good he'd had it.

The brothers discussed the idea of splitting up, to each look for the champion separately, but they'd done so much together in their lives that they were like the two hands of one body.

Separate, each was a hard worker who got the job done. But keep them together and boy-howdy-Mister you got your money's worth. More than one foreman was sorry to see them pick up and go after a twelve day stay.

Of course they always kept the Lord's Day holy and took the Sabbath for rest and church.

That was one thing Rembrandt noticed about travelling. No matter where they went, big city, small town or frontier railhead, God was there. It might be a hundred-foot-high cathedral or a canvas tent pitched in a coolie camp, but somebody was always busy praying about something.

Whether it was on polished oak pews or stumps and boards, he, Pa and Uncle Thompson sat near the back to hear the service. They tried to be humble in the Lord's house, even when the Lord's house was pretty humble itself.

And there was no napping when you sat between those two. Rembrandt heard every word every preacher said in three states before Pa passed. Plus eight more before that broken hip put Uncle Thompson off the schedule.

Some of the things he heard spoke to his heart. Some made him see that even preachers could be goddamned fools.

Not that he shared that particular observation with Pa or Uncle Thompson. They might say it themselves, but Rembrandt's britches weren't big enough just yet to speak ill of a man of God, fool or no.

Some might think that it was saying such a thing out loud that led to Pa's passing.

The three of them had been working on the puzzle of how hobo signs could not just tell you things, but could change the things themselves. It was exciting and Rembrandt felt like one of the three musketeers from that French book.

Uncle Thompson was all for trying out new things with the hobo signs and he had one idea that he wouldn't let go of.

"I want to try making a sign on my body," he said. "Just to see if it'll work."

That made Pa mad as hell.

"That's the Black Bottle Man's way of doing things," Pa said.

It was what Annie had done to her and Billy — drawing signs on their bodies with the ink from the black bottle. Pa didn't mention what Aunt *Emma* had done. That would've been too hurtful to Uncle Thompson.

"Look at what came of that," Pa said. "Families broke up. Immortal souls in danger of eternal damnation."

Thompson would keep quiet about the idea for a piece, and then up it would come again.

Until one Sunday, the last day of February 1928, when they went to a service in a brand-new clapboard church in Washington State, built so close to the Strait of Juan de Fuca that you could smell the Pacific Ocean the whole time through.

Rembrandt thought Pa and Thompson must have had the same effect on ministers that later got stuck to him, because it was one hell of a sermon.

The young preacher had the bit in his teeth about *Leviticus 19:28* — the one that forbid folks from making marks on their bodies. Rembrandt thought it was a funny coincidence that here it was 1928 and the preacher was so fired up about *19:28*.

He was a handsome man, that preacher. His hair was black, all flat and shiny with Brilliantine. You'd think he'd been anointed by the Lord himself.

"Anyone who makes a mark on their body," he said, "is damned to Hell. No ifs, buts or thank-you-Ma'ams."

You could see how that would put Pa and Uncle Thompson in mind of their quarrel. And how it would make it look like even trying to save Annie's and Emma's immortal souls was crazy.

If the man had said it once, it might have passed by, like a fishbone that almost got caught in your throat. But on that fine salt-scented Sunday morning, that preacher beat his pulpit with *Leviticus 19:28* until you thought the Lord had had nothing else to say.

A red flush appeared above Pa's collar and it wasn't long before his face was purple from holding his tongue. The preacher must have noticed, because soon he was screaming right at Pa, Uncle Thompson and Rembrandt. Then Pa spoke up.

"You're wrong, preacher," he said.

And quoted chapter and verse from Revelations about angels and such that had words marked on their bodies. He spoke like a man trying to convince those guarding the pearly gates to please let Annie and Emma into Heaven.

Rembrandt hadn't known that Pa had studied up on this so close. He guessed it made all the difference to Pa — whether he'd done right by his brother and his son, risking their souls to save Annie's and Emma's.

But the slicked-back preacher was adamant.

"You can commit any other sin and be forgiven," he said, "but make a mark on your body and you're damned without hope."

Right then and there Rembrandt knew that he'd study that Book like Pa had, until he knew all the funny little corners where the mean, small-minded people like to hide.

Then the preacher closed his Bible like the Final Trump was at hand and came stalking down the aisle. It made Rembrandt feel sick and flushed. Everybody in the church turned and looked at them. There were so many eyes, and they were all so self-righteous.

He wanted to say, "Those are my aunts the preacher says are beyond saving. My aunts that me, Pa, and Uncle Thompson have wagered our own hope of salvation to redeem against the terrible sins committed on a moonless night."

But he couldn't. He felt like Shadrack in the furnace. There was a fire blazing in that church and he was in it.

If he'd known what was coming, he would've done something, anything to change what happened next. He would've fallen to the floor and spoken in tongues. He would've jumped up and shouted, "Hallelujah! I've been saved!"

But he didn't know, so he just sat there, wishing he were invisible.

That's when Pa stood up.

To Rembrandt, looking up at Pa, it felt like the Archangel Michael was there, ready to do some smiting. But even then Pa thought of Rembrandt first. He put his hand on his son's shoulder, handed Thompson his hat and said, "Take the boy outside and get out of town."

Later, Rembrandt thought that somehow the Black Bottle Man must have cheated. They'd always kept the bargain of moving on before the thirteenth day. But there was something different about that particular Sunday.

It was the *29th* day of February 1928. A Leap Year.

Maybe that threw them off the schedule. Or maybe the Black Bottle Man's Pact had some tricky lawyer words to make it all come out wrong.

It must have been then that Pa realized that the Black Bottle Man was there, inside that preacher, inside those people.

Stirring them up, making them hate themselves until they were ready to do violence to others.

Rembrandt felt Uncle Thompson's big hands on his arms, pulling him out through the double-doors of that clapboard church, into a yellow sun-shine morning where you wouldn't believe that such things could happen.

Thompson stood on the new church-house steps, his pocket-knife out, hands twitching, trying to think of a hobo sign he could mark on the church to make things right.

"Stupid fool!" he cursed. "I just can't think."

Then they heard Pa yelling, "Run! Run!"

And fighting those people — those regular, normal people who'd gotten up that Sunday morning and put on their best, to sing hymns, to say "Hey" to their neighbours, and to praise the Lord.

Uncle Thompson pulled Rembrandt away and they ran.

At the edge of town Thompson got the two of them on a freight train headed south. They stopped in the next town and waited for Pa. Rembrandt felt all shivery and hollow inside but he held back the tears, trying to be a man.

"Maybe if I don't cry my pa will be alright."

"Dear God," he prayed. "If only You'll let Pa be alright, I'll never cry again in my whole life."

But word came that something bad had happened at the new church in the town next up the line.

Soon he and Uncle Thompson started learning how to make their own skin-signs.

Leviticus be damned.

9   Gail — 2007

GAIL IS HAPPY.

The County General Hospital doesn't want to keep her any more than she wants to be kept. The cut on her arm has been cleaned, stitched and bandaged, neat and tidy.

"Thank you, ladies." She nods her approval to the nurses on her way out. Let no one say she doesn't appreciate a job well done.

A matronly woman from social services makes a token effort to catch up with her, but Gail is out the door before Madam S.S. makes it past the starting gate.

There are police cars parked near the emergency room doors so Gail slips along the wall and around a corner. She doesn't think that Badge Number 3-5-9 will try to catch her again today, but there might be extenuating circumstances.

That's a phrase Gail loves. Extenuating circumstances. It's the Swiss Army knife of excuses. It fits any occasion and every event.

"I'm sorry, I couldn't take my medication due to extenuating circumstances."

"Your child was shot during a school hostage taking? Extenuating circumstances."

It leaves the details of guilt nice and vague. After all who wouldn't love to explain to everyone, over and over, why after being held at gunpoint for fifty-six hours without sleep, in a room filled with your terrified grade three music students, why you would choose to warn the hostage-taker when the nice policeman outside the window is trying to get you to move "OUT OF THE GOD-DAMN WAY!"

Nope — extenuating circumstances. It rolls off the tongue.

One of the doctors told Gail all about the Stockholm Syndrome. How people in a crisis will bond to the person in power, even when that person is the bad guy.

It all makes perfect sense — for other people. But not for Gail.

She loved her students. Everyone said so. And her students loved her back.

So how, after all those years of loving those kids and being loved in return could she have done anything that would cause them any harm?

The answer is clear.

It was all her fault. Because of extenuating circumstances.

10 Rembrandt —— 1927

THE MORNING AFTER, all the adults knew what Aunt Annie had done to Uncle Billy.

If the ink marks had only been on her, she might have kept it secret for a long time. Possibly until the baby was ready for birthing. Maybe even past that if she was extra careful.

People's bodies weren't on display in those days the way they are now. Clothes covered everything save face and hands, even when the mercury climbed to a hundred or more. And as far as marital relations were concerned, there was many a man who never saw the bare body of a wife who gave him eight or ten children.

"It" was something done after the lamp was blown out, under the covers, sometimes with three or four layers of sleeping clothes separating the two.

"It" was spoken of in euphemisms that danced around the subject like a country doctor's wife, fishing for her husband's fee.

"Congress," the doctors back east called it. Made you wonder what the heck they were up to, down in the Washington Capital.

How farm people could ignore all the "congress" that took place out in the barnyard was a miracle of human willful blindness. Not only the birds and the bees and the sycamore trees, but the cattle, the horses, the pigs, the goats, the sheep and every other creature God sent to Noah had its time for congress.

Polite folk — which means everybody except the little ones who didn't know better — did not mention... S — E — X.

But of course there was no hiding what Annie had done to Billy, *from* Billy.

He'd staggered out of their house in just his union suit and boots to find his morning relief in the outhouse. It wasn't proper for him to come out like that, with just one layer of clothes on him, even though strictly speaking the only parts not covered were the standard ones, face and hands.

But with the return to drinking he had become less concerned with what folks thought about him than he ought.

Their outhouse had the usual features of course. First, a well-sanded wooden plank seat, with a hole cut to your liking.

Young Rembrandt had used all of the Three Farms outhouses at one time or another and had his own personal favourite. It was not Uncle Billy's and Aunt Annie's. The hole in theirs was cut much too big for a boy of ten and it made him fear he might fall right through if he wasn't careful.

Second, there was the "material." What you used afterwards. That was a page torn out of a Sears or Eaton's catalogue, saved just for such a purpose.

Once, when Rembrandt was in town at Christmas time, visiting at a house that belonged to some rich folks, he'd had to use their outhouse. They had the fanciest "material" he'd ever seen. In place of the catalogue was a stack of little green squares of some kind of slippery-smooth paper. Each piece looked like it had been crumpled up and then smoothed out again.

Later, when it was time to go, the lady of the house gave Rembrandt a gift; a real treat in those days: a Japanese orange. That's when he knew where the "material" had come from, because the orange she handed him was wrapped in the special green paper.

In every season an outhouse held a way of taking a prideful body down a notch. In winter there was the cold that nips and the wind that slips through every crack. It took a positive act of will to drop your pants at forty below.

In summer there was the Sun.

Now the Sun is impartial. It shines on every place, in an even-handed fashion. But opening the door to a well-used outhouse in summertime would make you think the Sun had a particular liking for the place.

An outhouse in summer was not a place you tarried in, even in the cooler parts of the early morning. And Uncle Billy had missed the early morning by several hours.

Also, in summer there are the flies. And where there are flies, there are spiders. Looking down through the outhouse hole you could see them sitting in their caves, woven special to give them a place to hide. Big and ugly, they tended their webs, their bodies swollen with all the flies they could eat.

It made the idea of sitting down unattractive to say the least. And the prospect of dangling your privates down into that hole had a skin-crawling quality to be had nowhere else in the realm of human experience. The general result was that in the summer, many folks did not so much sit on the hole, as hover, like an East Indian swami preparing for his next feat, guaranteed to amaze the foreign traveller.

And in the hovering, eyes—which normally did not stray below the waist-line—were firmly fixed on the events taking place below.

So it was on that well-lit morning, after a night when the moon was not at her post to see the things that Aunt Annie (and Aunt Emma) had done, that Uncle Billy discovered strange lines and signs drawn on places where they should not have been.

11   Gail's Raymond — 2007

RAYMOND BREWER is a good man, mostly.

He has his flaws. A weakness for watching the early episodes of each season of American Idol. He's so sorry for those people. And a tendency to leave bigger tips if the waitress is cute. Not that he ever intends anything by it.

But for the most part he is a man worthy of his wife's love. And it is her love that he misses most in his life.

Gail was the best. They'd been lucky to find each other in the big world and they both had known it.

The hostage-taking had terrified Ray. After the shooting, the doctors kept Gail sedated for several days. Days during which she could not even speak. Days when Officer Slack told the hungry media over and over how the whole shooting mess was her fault.

"The guy was asleep," Slack claimed. "All I needed the lady to do was to move out of the way and 'Bang!' It all would've been over."

"But instead," he said, "she stands in the way and wakes the son-of-a-bitch up."

Ray had to defend her.

"Slack is crazy," he said. "There's no way Gail would do something like that."

He believed every word and wouldn't back down, even when Slack threatened to sue.

Lots of people backed Ray up. There were letters to the newspaper from people who knew Gail.

"She's a saint," they said. "She loves those kids."

Soon Ray was on national television. Theirs was a *cause célèbre*. People prayed for them. Until Gail woke up.

⚜

Things got so far out-of-hand that Ray agreed to let the news cameras be there when Gail was woken up. So the world would know that the first words out of her mouth were a flat denial of Officer Slack's accusations.

The doctors felt she was past the worst of the shock and let the medication wear off.

Ray sat at her hospital bedside, clasping her hand in his. It was like every bad soap opera you've ever seen, doing the "coma-victim awakens" bit. Only this was truly a tragedy.

Gail's eyes opened to see Ray's face.

"You're okay," he reassured her.

She looked at all the cameras and asked the question that would damn her.

"Is Andy okay?"

"Andy?" Ray echoed.

One of the reporters piped up, "Andy...Moore? Andrew Franklin Moore?"

"Yes," Gail replied. "Is Andy okay?"

Ray felt the floor fall away. Andrew Franklin Moore was the man who'd taken Gail and the children hostage.

Her question shocked the room into silence. That lasted all of five seconds. Then the reporters' questions came like knives. Ray was too stunned to react. Gail was defenceless and he just sat there.

Only his mother-in-law, Louise, a tiny nervous woman who never said boo, fought back. Her ferocious counterattack set

44

the swarming news-people back on their heels. By the time she was done the room was cleared of people and equipment. It probably took a year off of her life.

"Ray," Gail asked again, "how's Andy?"

He didn't have it in him to answer. Instead, in a hushed voice her mother gave Gail the news.

"Andrew Moore was shot and killed at the scene by Officer Slack," Louise said.

Gail didn't hear the rest. About the four children shot by Moore, one fatally. She couldn't hear it. Because she was crying.

Weeping over the death of Andrew Franklin Moore.

12 Rembrandt — 1927

WHEN UNCLE BILLY FOUND AUNT ANNIE, she was over in Ma's summer kitchen helping Ma and Aunt Emma with some early canning.

In the summer, putting up food was a full time occupation for the women. With no cash to spare for such frivolous things as tinned goods, it was put up your own food or starve come winter. It was the same for all the farm families. Even folks who lived and worked in town put up a cellar full of pickles, jams and jellies along with sacks of potatoes, carrots and more.

Of the three ladies, Rembrandt's ma was the best canner. The other two women were always careful to open their jars well before people came for a meal, just to make sure everything had the good, wholesome smell it ought to.

"But your ma," Pa claimed, "has never opened a bad jar of canning in all the years of our marriage."

Pa liked to tease Ma that she had "The Touch."

"It's a family gift, passed down from her ma and her ma's ma, and all the way back to Mother Eve."

"I'll eat anything your ma hands me," he said at the supper table, "provided it's not an apple."

Then he'd wink at Ma and say, "With no sister in Rembrandt's generation, maybe it's him who'll have The Touch."

"Who knows," Pa would say to the boy, "you might make a fine canner."

To which Ma said, "I'll give you a 'touch' all right," and showed him her cast-iron frying pan.

⚜

So when Uncle Billy slammed through the door into the summer kitchen there was a well-fed fire in the wood stove and pans of scalding hot water on top, ready to blanch the early vegetables and sterilize the jars and lids.

Like a good boy, young Rembrandt was outside.

"Stay out from underfoot," Ma had said, "but near enough to hear if we need you to fetch a pail of water from the drinking well."

Summer canning was hot, humid work that would make anybody cranky. Usually the women took the bad with the good and passed the time chatting about nothing much at all.

"Here's a funny looking cucumber," one might say, or, "This'll sure taste good come winter," just to take their minds off the little scalds and burns that came with canning.

But today, long before Uncle Billy raised Cain, young Rembrandt could sense a wall between his ma and the other two women. It was like she was on the outside and the two of them were on the in.

The aunts had a shared secret. A secret that made Emma laugh at the oddest places and made Annie mad at the same ones. Rembrandt was puzzled and from the way she got all quiet, he could tell Ma was too.

Uncle Billy marched past his nephew without so much as a "Good morning." He was still in his long-johns and boots and Rembrandt thought that the women would have something to say about that. But there he was wrong.

For a long moment, but for the snap of the fire and the hiss of water pans heating, the summer kitchen was silent.

47

Ma must have guessed at how serious things were, because she called out to Rembrandt. "Go fetch your pa and Uncle Thompson — and right now!"

Her tone sent him running as fast as he could go.

He missed whatever words were exchanged between Uncle Billy and the three women but when he got back, trailing Pa and Thompson, there was Ma standing with a big pan of scalding hot water in her hands, looking like she might throw it on Billy if he didn't step back.

"Pa," Ma called out, her eyes fixed on Uncle Billy's face, "you tell Rembrandt to run on over to the Cunninghams' and stay there 'til we come fetch him."

She didn't know the boy was standing right there, watching.

"Rembrandt, you get," Pa said, and he got.

It wasn't until the next day that Pa came to fetch him home.

Even though they lived two sections away, the Cunninghams were good neighbours and had no trouble fitting another boy into their brood for a meal or a night's sleep. They never even asked why Rembrandt's folks had sent him.

Mrs. Cunningham just said, "More water in the soup and there's plenty to go around."

⚜

Next day, Pa seemed different when they were walking home. Like he'd been scalded himself yesterday and was worried he might get scalded again today.

A couple of times he just stopped and gave Rembrandt a hug. That worried the boy more than a whack on the pants ever would've.

When they got home, the living arrangements were different.

"You've still got your place with your ma and me," Pa said, "but Uncle Thompson is going to live alone in his house now. Uncle Billy has left and the aunts are living in what had been Annie's and Billy's home."

It couldn't have been more topsy-turvy than San Francisco after the earthquake. But later, after the Black Bottle Man came to visit Three Farms, even the rubble of their lives was knocked down.

13 Gail — 2007

THE FILM FOOTAGE OF — "IS ANDY OKAY?" — aired again and again. Stills of Gail's bewildered face splashed across the tabloids, and each iteration soiled her soul anew.

"Please make it stop Raymond," his mother-in-law, Louise asked. "An injunction, something, anything."

But their lawyer said it couldn't be done. "Freedom of the press, you know."

Only when the endless news-cycle had picked its teeth with their bones did the instant replay of the end of their lives stop.

Officer Slack was magnanimous in his vindication.

"I understand how a husband would defend his wife," he said. "Now that the truth is out, so long as Mr. Brewer apologizes publicly, I'll drop the slander lawsuit."

Sadly, the making of a public apology was not considered sufficiently newsworthy to merit the national attention that Gail's hospital-bed revelation had received. Ray's apology ran on the local news once, and that was it.

The fact is, Raymond was sorry. He meant it when he told the camera how, "Gail was a good person caught in impossible circumstances."

And, "I wish I'd never opened my big, stupid mouth."

But the nation that slavered over —"Is Andy okay?" — didn't see that apology. So the nation went on believing that Raymond and Gail Brewer were heartless liars and worse.

14 Rembrandt — 1927

LOSING EMMA AND THEN THREE FARMS shook Uncle Thompson pretty hard. But travelling with Pa and Rembrandt, and being able to talk a little bit about it every day kept him from giving into despair.

As it still is with men today, Thompson couldn't come right out with his hurt all at once and get it on the outside, the way a wise woman would've.

The first few days after they left Three Farms the two men didn't say much at all.

Just a couple of words at a time, meant to convey information about concrete things like, "Saskatoons there..." to point out some roadside berry bushes they could pick to fill Rembrandt's hollow leg.

In happier times that's what Uncle Thompson said about Rembrandt's appetite.

"I'm sure that boy has a hollow leg."

Those evenings when Rembrandt had sat down to supper at Uncle Thompson and Aunt Emma's table, they'd always had two extra helpings: one for him, and one for his hollow leg.

Of the Three Farms men, Pa, Billy, and Thompson, it was his Uncle Thompson who'd been most like a playmate to Rembrandt. The youngest adult at Three Farms, Thompson had been the one to put down his pitchfork after a full day's work and pick up a ball and glove to play catch with the boy, never missing a beat.

And it was his Uncle Thompson who understood about chasing dust devils.

From the time he could toddle Rembrandt loved to run after the swirls of dust and straw that would rise up out of nowhere on a late August afternoon.

It made his ma mad enough to spit, seeing the boy do that, but for all her fussing she never once laid a hand to his bottom about it.

They'd be reaping up in the north-forty, or down haying the meadow, with the clouds piled up, white and purple-black all the way to Heaven. How something could be both so pure and white, and so dark and threatening at the same time was a marvel. It was like God was showing you how he felt that day.

Pa said, "Working in a field just seems to call the prayers out of a man. Praying it'll rain in the spring, for the crops to grow. Praying it won't in August, so the stooks can dry. Praying all summer long that the hail will pass you by, or at least not flatten everything."

Young Rembrandt said, "God sure must like praying Pa, 'cause he made so many fields."

They'd be stooking the grain, wrapping a twist of straw around the waist of a bundle of wheat so that it could stand up and keep the kernels dry, ready for when the threshing gang would come. Then a hot breath of wind would find its own tail and a dust devil would stir.

Spotting one always made young Rembrandt laugh. That was part of what made Ma mad and part of what made her hold that temper. Mad because there was work to be done, but how could you be mad at a boy who laughed at the Devil?

Uncle Thompson was a mischief. When Rembrandt was little, on hearing that laugh, Thompson would drop his stook unfinished and scoop the boy up to run after every single dust devil. Carrying the boy must have slowed him down some, because they never caught one together.

When Rembrandt was a bit older and steady on his feet, he and his uncle would race, each trying to be the first to catch a piece of straw out of the spinning wind.

Thompson wasn't one of those uncles who held back or faked a sore knee to let his nephew win a race. He went full bore, sprinting like a pronghorn.

"All ass and elbows," Uncle Billy called it.

You never knew which of the two would have a head-start. A dust devil might be closer to one than the other, but Rembrandt's laugh was always their starter's pistol. If Thompson saw it first, he'd wait until the boy heard the puff of wind, saw their target, and gave the signal.

Because he went all out, and being a grown man, most times Uncle Thompson won the race. He'd stand in the dust devil's center with his hair dancing and his eyes closed to keep the dirt out, reaching up to catch a golden piece of straw.

One year, when the threshing gang came to work at Three Farms, a man who'd come all the way from Australia saw the two of them doing this. He told Rembrandt that where he came from the dust devils were called "willy-willy."

Thereafter, when the boy raced for a dust devil he'd call out, "Willy-willy!"

Uncle Thompson took to saying it as well, because even grown men like the joke of saying something a little bit rude in front of the women.

The others understood. It was their own joke, Rembrandt's and Thompson's, and no one else could share in it.

But now on the road, much of the play had gone out of Uncle Thompson, leeched away by the loss of his wife and the place he had poured so much of himself into.

Ma had said, "You never truly own a farm. It's more like it owns you."

Or maybe it's like a baby is to a woman: something to be cared for and nurtured; that grows over time into part what you'd hoped for, and part what it is, itself.

After a few quiet days of travelling, it was Three Farms that Uncle Thompson was able to talk about first. It would be a long time before he would even consider discussing the black magic their sister, Annie had done. Who knew if he'd ever be able to speak about how his wife, Emma had joined in too?

"I'm sure your ma will be able to sell Three Farms for a good price," Thompson let on. "The houses are well-made, and tight against the winter. Each has good water for both house and barn, and anyone starting out would think farming was easy, stepping onto land that was so well broke."

It sounded like this was meant to reassure Rembrandt's pa, but the boy could see that his uncle drew a positive comfort out of the idea that what he and his kin had created out of the raw gifts of the earth would be valued by someone else, and that a new family might thrive where others had faltered.

"Even if she can't sell the farms right away," Thompson said, "we've good crops standing in the fields, and if the prices are half-ways decent your ma will clear enough after paying the threshing gang to get back east to her kin with money to spare."

"She'll be fine," Thompson said. "Cash-wise."

Young Rembrandt heard Pa agree with everything Thompson said, letting the younger man have the time and space to rebuild himself.

In later years, Rembrandt thought that of the two, his father had been the luckier man. His wife hadn't betrayed him; hadn't let the sly promises of the Black Bottle Man put them asunder.

He could see that for Pa, leaving Ma behind was a kind of sacrament to their marriage, not a breaking of their vows. His parents bore their duty to kin like battle flags. Fighting for Annie and Emma's souls was right because they were family.

"Besides," Pa said, "how could I ever stand in front of Saint Peter and own up to letting the Devil win without a fight?"

15 Three Farms — 1927

IT WAS FIVE WEEKS TO THE DAY from when Uncle Billy left, that the Black Bottle Man came to Three Farms. Five weeks of awkward meals and morning sickness. Because those two babies sure took.

"The letter promised results," Ma said to the women, "and you've got no reason to complain on that account."

The house the other two women shared took on the unpleasant smell of morning sick-ups. Uncle Thompson couldn't bring himself to go near the place, so Rembrandt carried each day's results far away from the houses and buried that vomit in the ground.

In the beginning, the six of them gathered for the evening meal at Ma and Pa's house. It was neutral territory and the appearance of peace could be set out like a decoy hoping to lure in the real thing. But it wasn't long before the saying of grace became a bone of contention.

Ma would give thanks to the Lord and you'd hear a mutter at the table. So soft it was, that with your head bowed and your eyes closed, you couldn't tell who said it. And no one would own up to it.

Rembrandt knew it wasn't him. He suspected it might be Emma, or maybe Annie. But they both denied it. Uncle Thompson swore on the Holy Spirit that it wasn't him.

Whoever said it, it didn't stop. And every time it happened, the meal would taste sour. Not because the food was bad, not at Ma's table, but because mocking the Lord was something to put a bad taste in your mouth.

So without anyone saying they ought to, Annie and Emma stopped coming. They did for themselves and stayed in Billy's old house, the south house.

Rembrandt could see Uncle Thompson act like that direction — south — didn't exist anymore. If Thompson had to walk south across his yard, his head was down, watching his steps.

The boy felt bad for his aunts, but the muttering at grace stopped, and for a while supper-time began to feel almost normal again.

⋙

The day the Black Bottle Man came, Ma had sent Rembrandt across the roads with loaves of fresh bread, one for Thompson and two for the women in the south house.

Ma was always careful to speak of the two women in a respectful way, always called them "Your Aunt Annie and Aunt Emma." But in Rembrandt's mind, they had become "the women in the south house."

The sky was a dome of blue, untouched by clouds — like God wasn't giving any hints about how He felt that day.

Returning from the south house, the boy saw something raising dust down the east road. It might have been a team and buckboard, or it might have been a dust devil with a liking for the road. He shaded his brow. He had sharp eyes and ran to tell his pa that a man was coming long before the horses blew into the yard.

By that time Pa, Thompson and Rembrandt were standing in front of the south house. No one said that that was where they needed to be, but that was where they were just the same. They might have been three instead of three hundred, but they held that ground like Spartans.

The team was nothing special. Looked to Rembrandt like horses he knew from the livery in town. So was the buckboard.

The man was special though. He'd come a long way down a dirt road in summer, but his dark coat was as clean as you please.

He had a "glad-ta-meet-ya" smile Rembrandt never saw again, save the once, on that President everyone seemed to trust so much.

"You're not welcome here, Satan," Pa said. He saw things clearly and wasn't one to mince words.

The man's gaze slid over Pa and climbed the porch of the south house to the second-storey windows. Rembrandt turned to see his aunts peeking out from behind the white lace curtains, like brides-to-be.

"I think you're wrong, mister," the stranger replied.

The dark-coated man sat back and the wagon's seat-springs gave him a squeaky little bounce.

Ma joined them in a rush, brandishing the family Bible that her folks had cherished all the way back, time out of mind, like a sword. It was big and leather bound, heavy with brass corners. A Book meant to last.

Seeing that, the man gave them a barn-cat look.

"I belong here," he said. "That Book's got no hold over me today."

Ma, not one to believe the Devil's lies, flung that Bible at him like David's slingshot come alive. And it would've nailed him too, if he hadn't snatched it out of the air, snake-fast.

In his hands it looked small and fragile. He flipped Ma's Bible open and with fingers long and greasy, tore out a couple of pages. One he popped into his mouth like a just-done slice of bread. The balls of his eyes squeezed back into his head the way a toad's do when it's swallowing a mealworm. The other page he smoothed out on his knee. He let the Good Book fall to the ground, in the dirt behind the horses.

"That wasn't very nice," the man said, "but..."

He liked that word so much he said it again. "But...I'm always willing to bargain."

He flourished a steel-nibbed pen. The kind they used down at the courthouse to sign papers that put people inside jails that weren't fit for a dog.

That's when Pa and Thompson made their deal.

"The Pact," the Black Bottle Man called it.

"Annie and Emma will leave Three Farms, never to return. I insist on that."

"In their time they will have those two babies, or not, as Nature sees fit, and the babies will be free of taint."

Ma surrendered a sigh of relief at that news.

"In return, I will get my Black Bottle back. The souls of the two women belong to me when they die though. They've done witchcraft and their souls are rightfully mine. To have any chance to change that, you'll have to put up something worth my while. And gentlemen, the only valid currency at this poker table is souls."

Pa did the talking. He'd look at Thompson and get a nod on the major points.

"Here's our offer," Pa said. "Thompson and I will put up our own souls as forfeit if we fail. In our lifetimes we'll find a champion who can beat you, Satan. If we fail, you get all four souls: aunts' and brothers' both."

Rembrandt thought it was a fair offer, but the Black Bottle Man was a wheedler.

"I've done these bargains since Moses was a pup," he said, "and I want the game to be more...fun.

"Conditions," he said. "Conditions make the sport worth the time. My conditions are:

"A) The men cannot stay longer than twelve days in any one place, be it a city, town, village or farm house; twelve days, counted on the regular calendar, like the one for this year.

1927. If you don't move on according to the schedule, I get to do *something* to move you along.

"B) Pa and Thompson can put up as many champions as they want to. It makes no difference to me. But each one has to know who they're going to fight and agree that their soul will go into the pot as well. And,

"C) If, before Pa and Thompson die, their champion beats me, then all the souls bargained for will go to the arms of Lord Jesus when their time comes."

Pa worked that one over front and back, making sure there was no wiggle room for the Great Serpent. The Black Bottle Man made a big show over how clever Pa was, trying to flatter him into being stupid.

The two men were ready to shake on it, but the Devil wanted one more thing.

"I don't really have to agree to this. I'm only doing it out of my sense of fair play. What this Pact needs is some spice."

The man smiled over at Rembrandt and Ma.

"I want a third soul on the velvet."

Rembrandt saw his ma lick her lips, ready to put hers on offer. But he didn't give her the chance. Taking his father's elbow and drawing him down, he whispered into Pa's ear so quiet he was sure the Devil couldn't hear.

"I'm part of the cause, let me help with the cure."

Ma saw the lay of things and shook her head *No*. But Pa knew how it had to be.

"He's right, Ma," Pa said. "A woman can't join men travelling like that, moving every twelve days. There's a place in the world for moving men. For a woman, there's not."

"With Pa and Uncle Thompson along," Rembrandt said, "I'll be okay, Ma."

"If the Lord's willing," Thompson chimed in, "we'll do this quick and have things back to rights — or at least as right as they ever can be — before too much time has passed."

The boy's uncle crouched down and looked Rembrandt in the eye. How glad a man can be for a son, that was how Thompson looked at his nephew. They both nodded at Pa and he finished the bargain.

"The third soul on the table will be Rembrandt's. All previous conditions apply to him too. But...!"

Pa liked playing that word back at the Black Bottle Man. "But, you will guarantee that the boy's natural life will be the full four-score and ten years, *and,*" — this was where Pa twisted the Devil's tail — "and thirty days more."

The Black Bottle Man scowled, but "Done" was the answer.

The Pact complete, the black bottle that had started all the trouble appeared in the stranger's hands and with a jingle of harness he and the rig were gone back down the road.

Ma reclaimed the family Bible from where it lay in the dirt. It fell open to show where the pages had been torn out. *Leviticus* was gone.

16 Rembrandt — 1927

ANNIE AND EMMA WERE THE FIRST TO GO, packed and on their way within hours.

No one told Rembrandt where and he didn't ask. He would've said goodbye to them, but they must have been too ashamed to face him. It didn't matter much. He was doing this for Pa and Uncle Thompson, and to keep Ma safe.

The four of them that remained worked fast to get things ready.

In the twelve days allowed they laid up what firewood, feed and such that Ma would need for a while. Rembrandt listened while the men talked with her about what they could take and what to leave behind, where they might go and what kind of champion might beat the Devil.

The three adults had all grown up back east and thought the best hope for success would lie in the West.

"There are plenty of good folks back east," Pa said. "But their lives have gotten too easy."

"You'll need someone who's had a hard life," Ma said, "and been tested by the Lord."

So west it was. Pa knew where Ma would be, either here at Three Farms or in Montreal with her widowed father. He trusted her to explain the way things were and left it at that.

The morning they left Three Farms, Rembrandt walked around the place, trying to make pictures of it in his heart, and saying goodbye to the animals. He even said goodbye to the ugly, old spiders in the outhouse. After all, they were God's creatures too.

Then came a round of hugs with Ma, the like to squeeze the breath out of you.

Followed by a request for promises, "To be a good boy and... mind your manners."

Watching Ma let Pa go, that was harder than anything a boy should have to see. So Uncle Thompson took his hand and the two of them walked on ahead down the west road a pace.

"Your pa will catch up in a bit."

IN TACOMA, WASHINGTON Rembrandt learned to hate the smell of salmon.

Not long after Pa's death in the clapboard church, Tacoma was where he and Uncle Thompson made a stop and took jobs in a fish-canning factory to make ends meet.

In those days, factories hired plenty of eleven-year-old boys, and younger. Boys were small enough to fit inside the machinery, to clean the gears and such, and could stay there all day, even when the machines were running.

Pa's death must have rattled Uncle Thompson, because he didn't see how dangerous the work was going to be for his nephew. Thompson's job was outside, shovelling fish off the boats and he couldn't see what the boys had to do, so he didn't know until it was too late.

Salmon weren't a steady thing, so the factory only ran when the fish did. And when the salmon did run, it was one of God's own marvels to see. The rivers of Washington State were clean and cold, but when the salmon made their way upstream, heading for the spawning grounds, those rivers came alive.

Rembrandt could've watched for hours, so beautiful those fish were. And so intent too on rushing upstream to have congress that it seemed to excite the whole town, just to see how bad the fish wanted "it." But Rembrandt wasn't thinking about "it," when *it* happened.

At the dock, boats came in, two and three at a time. Thompson and other men scooped the fish up onto conveyor belts, headed into the cannery. So fresh were the salmon, most were still flopping. Newly arrived from their years exploring the ocean, salmon are a clean fish. But any fish has its coating of slime. It's like a second skin, protecting the fish from germs and helping it to swim through the water, extra easy.

So when the salmon came up the belts and in the cannery door, they brought tons and tons of slippery, gooey slime with them. And where that slime got into the machinery, it had to be scraped off. If it wasn't, belts would slip and production would stop.

If that happened, the owners would speak sternly to the cannery manager. The manager would yell at the line foremen. The foremen would scream at the mechanics and the mechanic's boys would get the mechanic's fists. It was a management style not now missed by most.

It was Rembrandt's job to clean the workings of a machine that bore the nasty name of "Iron Chink." It was so called because the machine had taken the jobs of many of the early Chinese immigrant workers. As little as they were paid, *it* worked for less.

Being the mechanic's boy for the Iron Chink was supposed to come with its own important tool, a long-handled wooden scraper. But some earlier boy had broken the scraper, so that now it was of the short-handled variety. This shortcoming did not matter to the mechanic, and that corporate policy was made clear to Rembrandt without need of a memo.

Life on the farm teaches a boy to work. And Rembrandt was a hard worker. But this was not the farm. Helping stook grain or weed the garden, you could pause for a moment to catch your breath or change your grip on the hoe. It didn't matter. Everyone knew that you were doing your part.

But the cannery machines were above all that human frailty.

Rembrandt and the short-handled scraper were placed where the needs of the machine dictated. The belts and metal moved on a fixed cycle. Every minute the Iron Chink paused, opened a gear-filled mouth and let the boy scrape off its whorish tongue.

A long-handled scraper would've let him achieve this task with only the usual level of risk. In some factories each year one in twenty boys lost a limb to the machinery. Another one in twenty died from it.

Taken together that was a one in ten chance. Compound that by the six years a boy might spend working inside the machinery before he won promotion to mechanic, and you had an attrition rate any Great War general would have found hard to beat.

The new child labour laws weren't popular with factory owners. They took decades to spread across Canada and the U.S. Most of those "progressive" laws only applied until you turned fourteen and enforcement was on par with the Ten Commandments: more honoured in the breach, as they say.

But the scraper's handle was not long. So every minute, when the maw opened Rembrandt's arm went in, up to the elbow.

It was a small piece of luck for Rembrandt that his uncle was working outside on the docks. If Thompson had been inside the cannery, it's unlikely that he would've heard the screams over the roar of the machines.

He was out of that boat and running up the conveyor itself before the moving gears released the boy's arm. Through the conveyor-belt door he came, salmon skittering under foot, following those cries. Shouldering the mechanic aside, he tore open the sheet-metal panel.

Thompson had lost his brother a score of days before. Now his nephew lay gasping on the slime-coated floor — like another gutted salmon — his right hand and arm a pulp of mangled muscle and bone.

18 Tacoma — 1928

ON A RESIDENTIAL STREET, down a piece from the cannery, a rough-looking man held a broken boy, like live models for Michelangelo's *Pieta*.

There'd been no help to be had at the factory. Thompson could've decked that stupid mechanic.

He looked at the first house. It was big and brick, likely built from the cannery's profits. His boot opened the gate and then announced to the occupants that someone was at the door. A hand pinched back a bay window curtain and half a face dared to show itself. It stayed where it was, watching.

"Help us!" Thompson cried. "Please, help us!"

The hand twitched the curtain closed but no one opened the door. No one here thought Rembrandt worth a dirtied floor.

After Rembrandt's pa had died, Thompson had scourged himself over what he could have done. Hindsight, the handmaiden of self-recrimination, had been a big help on that score.

The hobo signs had been new to Thompson on that bad Leap Year Sunday. They were still new to him in Tacoma, but this time he was prepared. He laid Rembrandt on the porch planks and with his pocket-knife scratched a stick-figure woman and three quick triangles on the varnished wooden door. The hobo sign for *a kind woman lives here.*

He tried to spit, to get the moisture he needed to rub on the sign, the way he had with *good fishin'* — to make it change the world. That sign had brought trout. He prayed that this one would bring a kind woman. But panic had left his mouth dry and no spit would come.

Blood dripped from the boy's arm. And though it felt like a line you couldn't re-cross, Thompson dipped his fingers into the red and spread it around the scraped symbol.

Then just like the first trout had hit that hook, the scratched door opened and an angel of mercy took them under her wing.

19 Tacoma — 1928

UPSTAIRS, THE ANGEL OF MERCY LAY the boy down on her second best bed. In a trice, a length of scarf and a hairbrush made a tourniquet at his elbow.

Trailing them up the stairs, Thompson saw a photograph of a younger version of this woman. In the picture she wore the white cap of one of Mrs. Nightingale's Sisters of Mercy.

"Please Lord," he prayed. "Let it be so."

It had been ten years since the Great War but the woman moved with a certainty born from experience.

"Stand here, sir." She pointed at the head of the bed. "Take this and be ready."

She handed over the tourniquet to his care.

A second woman hovered at the bedroom door, "tsking" like she'd suck the enamel off her front teeth. The Sister of Mercy grabbed the second woman's arm and the noise stopped.

"Mind me, Mrs. Jackson. Fetch my bag, the green one, from the front hall. And don't forget the bone saw."

Mrs. Jackson scuttled away, anxious to be shed of this errand, "tsking" at the blood spots on the front stairs carpet.

"Sister, the cannery—" Thompson began.

"Gears." She said it like a curse.

Scissoring the boy's torn sleeve away to the shoulder she lifted the arm to examine the damage.

"Your son — I can try to saw below the elbow, but it might be safer to take it off above."

The Sister waited.

Thompson's breath clawed his throat.

The Sister waited.

Mrs. Jackson entered.

Two items were dropped onto the bed.

Mrs. Jackson left and the Sister waited.

"Sir."

"No—"

"Sir—"

"No!"

Her chin jutted and she insisted.

"Sir—"

"Please...he's eleven."

"Gangrene—"

Thompson's pulse roared in his ears.

"Please, no!" It was more prayer than answer. His chest shook but no sound escaped.

The Sister picked something appalling up from the bed and set a steel bone-saw over on the bedside table.

"Later then...." She'd seen this before.

The Sister opened her green bag and extracted gauze, which she wrapped around and around the thin little arm. She showed Thompson how to loosen the tourniquet for a short time every half hour.

"Call me back when you're ready. I won't be far." She left, closing the door.

The boy's eyelids fluttered, but did not open.

"He looks so much like his pa," Thompson whispered. "How could I have let this happen?"

His tears, big and hot, splashed on Rembrandt's smooth young face. He touched the wet, wiping it away. It was such a beautiful face. The wet left a track on the boy's skin.

Before that bad Leap Year Sunday, Thompson had talked a lot about trying to make one of the hobo signs on his own skin. His brother had been dead set against it. It smacked too much of what Annie and Emma had done with the black bottle.

Rembrandt's pa had even quoted *Leviticus 19:28* at him. That had shut Thompson up for a bit, but he had come back with another idea. He wouldn't permanently mark himself. He'd just draw the picture with spit. If he didn't like it, a quick rub and it would be gone.

Rembrandt's pa had thought about that for a while, but he couldn't see all the ways of it, so he was still against it.

Now, Thompson dearly wished he had his brother's good counsel. He closed his eyes and tried to talk it through.

"Thompson, you're a blind man on old Noah's Ark, reaching out. You might find the lamb or you might find the tiger.

"There's a hobo sign for *'good doctor'*—

"But all a good doctor will do is take Rembrandt's arm, same as the Sister."

"Nothing else seems to fit. We're in the wilderness and I don't have forty years to find my way. God! I've been a good man. Even more, little Rembrandt is an innocent. What kind of a God would create folks willing to trade a boy's arm for a can of fish?"

Fish.

That seemed to echo back at Thompson.

"Fish."

It had been the first thing the hobo signs had given them, those trout-fish that had fed the whole camp.

"And — before the Cross —

"The great healer's secret symbol had been the sign of — a fish!"

Quickly, smearing his drying tears across Rembrandt's cheek Thompson made two curved lines, joined at one end and intersecting at the other.

A fish — the ancient symbol of the great healer.

20 Raymond — 2007

WEEKDAY MORNINGS ARE HARDEST FOR RAY.

The bedroom closet is still full of Gail.

On her bedside table a stack of novels linger but he cannot touch their untold stories. Putting them away would be too much like giving up. So they sit, collecting their daily dust.

When they'd first been married and money was tight, Gail taught Raymond the joys of porridge. How a bowl of cooked oats can become a delight to the senses. The secret is to let it stand for a minute, until the surface becomes a kind of skin covering the hot grain beneath. Then float a lake of cold milk on top and add an island of coarse brown sugar.

Your first spoonful shapes the porridge world. Milk plunges through the pierced surface pulling brown tendrils of dissolving sugar into the abyss.

With Gail gone now, Ray still makes porridge each morning. It keeps the taste of heartache fresh and that's just what he wants: to feel something.

Much of the rest of the day is numbed by work and the business of life — the mask of normality he wears to keep the world at bay.

After work, supper with Gail's mother, Louise, has become the ritual. With Gail's father taken by a mid-life crisis, they are both alone now. Raymond buys groceries and Louise cooks; a lamed parody of both their broken marriages.

Louise always cooks for three. After the meal, the dishes are cleared away and they undertake their daily mission. Months of practice have honed their skills and they can count on getting five out of seven evening meals into Gail's stomach. Some of the others are lost to bums or animals, or simply forgotten and left to spoil.

When making the delivery they're careful not to let Gail see their faces. Otherwise, it sets her off and she runs.

It's easy to find her again. Every weekday morning she can be found counting in front of the school. But it especially hurts Louise to see her daughter run away from her.

So Raymond bought two balaclavas: one for himself and one for Louise. So long as they refrain from speaking, Gail allows the masked people to leave a Styrofoam carton of food in her cardboard nest.

Husband and mother, they're a team. But there is one secret about all this that Raymond has never told Louise.

On Saturday and Sunday mornings he makes sure to get to Gail's hiding place early enough to give her breakfast.

It's always the same thing.

A bowl of porridge, with milk and brown sugar.

21 Rembrandt —— 1928

SOMETIMES YOU CAN LEARN A LOT by staying in bed.

Young Rembrandt learned that Mrs. Arlington was a widow and had no children of her own. That made him a little nervous at first, what with his aunts and all, but it seemed she'd made her own peace on that subject.

He learned that once upon a time, back in the days of the Great War, she was a nurse in France. He told her about Uncle Billy, who'd been in the Great War too and had said, "The nursing sisters were the bee's knees."

But despite his reasonable expectations, Mrs. Arlington didn't think she'd ever met Uncle Billy on the battlegrounds of Europe.

"There were an awful lot of people over there," Mrs. Arlington explained, "and we were awful busy."

Since the accident, she had let Rembrandt stay in her spare bedroom. It was about the fanciest place he'd ever seen. Nicer than even the Japanese orange lady's house.

The food was pretty good too, except since waking up Rembrandt had found he didn't much like salmon anymore. And Mrs. Arlington's sister-in-law, Mrs. Jackson, who did all the cooking, seemed to have an endless supply of the stuff.

But he minded his manners like Ma said and cleaned up his plate. Luckily, Uncle Thompson hadn't told them about his hollow leg, so he didn't have to cope with seconds.

For a nurse, Mrs. Arlington sure did worry a lot about bandages though. She kept coming into the spare bedroom to check on Rembrandt's arm and the way she looked at him, it was like she expected him to sprout wings and fly.

During his first visit, Uncle Thompson warned Rembrandt not to mention the hobo signs.

Tut! Who'd been the one who pricked his thumb at the hobo camp? Like he didn't know how to keep a secret?

Another thing he learned sitting in bed was that some adults spend a lot of time pretending they don't like each other, when anyone can see that they do. Like when Uncle Thompson was visiting — he didn't stay in Mrs. Arlington's house, that wouldn't be proper — he would sit on the edge of Rembrandt's bed, but only if Mrs. Arlington wasn't present.

The way his uncle leapt up when she came into the room would've made you think that the very idea that he'd ever touched a bed was something else he wanted to keep secret. Then the two of them both would make a big fuss over Rembrandt, saying things like —

"What a handsome boy he is." And,

"He sure likes it here."

— when Rembrandt was sure that they should have been using different pronouns, like "you" and "I."

It was like watching a couple of colts on the farm, all awkward and feisty, trying out legs that neither one of them was quite sure of. Then the other lady, Mrs. Jackson, would go "tsking" by, pretending to ignore this adolescent display of attraction, and Mrs. Arlington would suddenly remember a letter that needed posting.

Seeing those sparks between Mrs. Arlington and Uncle Thompson made Rembrandt think of his ma and pa.

Since she was good with letters and his arm was still sore, he asked Mrs. Arlington to help him write to his ma. He wanted to let her know what had happened to Pa.

It's hard, talking with a lump in your throat, but Mrs. Arlington was good at waiting for folks. Most grown-ups don't have the patience God gave a housefly, but she had a gift for just being quiet. It took them a couple of evenings to finish, but Rembrandt felt that his ma would want to know everything he could think to say. Ma's are like that.

He said some things about Pa and the clap-board church that gave away the secrets his uncle wanted to keep hidden from Mrs. Arlington, but when someone's just sitting there with a pen, ready to write down whatever you have to say, it's like there's a silent hole in the world that you've just got to fill up.

It made him wonder what else God might have had to say, if Moses had been as patient as Mrs. Arlington. An extra commandment or two sure could've saved a lot of trouble.

When they were done the letter, Mrs. Arlington put it in an envelope and promised to mail it to Ma's father in Montreal. It had been more than a year since they had walked down the west road away from Three Farms and it seemed likely that Ma would've sold the homesteads and gone back east by now.

Because he'd been asleep for a few days, due to the accident, it came as a surprise when Uncle Thompson said they had to leave. From the things Rembrandt had said in the letter to his ma, Mrs. Arlington must have understood that this was coming and didn't make a big to-do. Uncle Thompson was all set to give her a made-up story about why they had to go when it was clear the hurt arm wasn't finished healing. But she just looked at Uncle Thompson in her patient way and he stopped talking.

When the man and boy were ready to go, the three of them paused on the veranda where Rembrandt had come so close to dying. The scratches on the front door were gone, repaired by Thompson.

Mrs. Arlington gave Rembrandt a hug, like she needed to stand in for his ma, if only for a minute. Then the two adults looked everywhere but at each other.

Thompson stammered out his, "Thanks."

And Mrs. Arlington said, "You're welcome."

Then Rembrandt and Uncle Thompson walked down the porch steps and out the gate.

⚜

On their way out of town they passed the docks and Thompson caught Rembrandt smiling at the canning factory.

"What could you possibly find funny about that horrible place?"

"Well," Rembrandt said, "I think maybe Pa was wrong. That thing he used to say to Ma about me at the dinner table?

"It doesn't look like I've got Ma's 'touch' for canning, after all."

22 Rembrandt — 2007

AN ASPHALT WIND STIRS Old Rembrandt's thin white hair. His first full day in this city has slipped away. Night has fallen hours before, but the windows of Television City deny this street corner any chance of solitude.

It's too early to return to the Sally Ann. Sleep doesn't come easy anymore and with luck the hall may cool a bit from the day's heat.

Thirty televisions face him through big plate-glass windows. Like a community choir, most are in tune but a few lesser lights are on display just to show how good the best ones really are.

A blue neon sign eulogizes the death of the classroom spelling-bee, proclaiming that the store manager has "E-Z credit 4-U."

The store is closed but Rembrandt is not alone. Nearby a street-woman also watches the display, swaying to some inner dirge while evening traffic lurches past.

Bolted high up the wall a caged speaker shares a thin version of the soundtrack, the dialogue and music flattened and cracked with distortion.

The sets play the final act of a made-for-television movie in unison, like a Greek chorus re-enacting a tragedy. It claims to be the true-life story of some people called "Andy and Gail."

Whatever basis in truth the film may have has been massaged to make way for the mandatory uplifting conclusion. Somehow the heroine finds the strength to overcome the bad man's fatal attraction and together, she and a handsome police officer prevent a terrible tragedy, all while finding true love in each other's arms.

Repeated over thirty big screens it bathes Rembrandt and the street-woman in a sickly, xanthic light.

The show ends and the street-woman seems unduly touched by the saccharin story. She turns away, shoulders hunched to hold some private pain within herself, a veteran laboring across a re-visited battlefield.

There is a quality to pain that attracts attention: the attention of those who wish to help, and the attention of those who enjoy the distress of others. Rembrandt respects the right to private pain and would never have spoken to the street-woman, save for the sharks.

Boys they are, but sharks too. He sees them coming down the street, five boys in their late teens, the masters of all they survey. Nice clothes, well groomed, they are privileged without the sense to know it.

In turning away, the street-woman has set course into a storm she fails to see. But he can see it. And it looks to be a bad one.

There are unintended consequences to every act of kindness or bravery. It is probably best that we can never foresee what will come from what we do. Perhaps that's why people so seldom see God's hand in the world. An omniscient God would see all the pain that even His most well-intentioned choice would cause.

But unintended consequences or no, Rembrandt cannot stand idly by and watch this scene unfold. In his bag of tricks is a hobo sign he has not used in over seven decades. Not because it is ineffective, but because it is all too potent.

It is, *police here*.

Rembrandt first made that hobo sign soon after Uncle Thompson died in Montana. He was fifteen and scared. Both his pa and Uncle Thompson were gone and the road had more than its share of men willing to beat you senseless just because it made them feel big for a little while. But as he learned back then, there are worse things than a beating.

23 Rembrandt — 1932

AFTER WORD ABOUT UNCLE THOMPSON reached Rembrandt in Missoula, he was uncertain about which way to turn. He felt like those fishermen at Galilee: at sea and afraid.

So when some men said that they were going on down the line, he let himself be swept along. He'd lost track of time and knew the twelfth day must be coming up soon. So it would be a good idea to move on again. It would give him time to think on what he should do.

Hobos had two simple rules. When things get tough you take care of your kin. And you stand up for your friends.

But these men were not Rembrandt's kin. And they were not his friends.

So when Slick Willy Palmer decided he wanted to beat the tar out of a wet-behind-the-ears boy, there was no one there to stand up for Rembrandt but himself.

24 Slick Willy Palmer —— 1932

SLICK WILLY PALMER enjoyed being king.

He had the size needed to be a tool push, wildcatting in the Texas oil fields. Then a broken pipe took his left eye.

Drink and dope for the pain used up his money and then an uppity Chinese made the mistake of looking at him wrong. It was, as Willy put it, "A hell of a world when a white man can't even kill a Chink without having to leave town."

The sheriff knew better than to chase Willy farther than the city limits. But the killing put him on the road, and six months on the move taught him plenty about the hobo camps.

His royal formula was simple. Find a new camp. Spot a loner. Sucker punch the son-of-a-bitch and then kick the hell out of him. That got everyone's attention.

A circle of roadmen would form, watching. That was the moment he loved best. Like a matador facing the bull. That was the perfect moment, when a camp full of men who've seen you do violence must decide what to do.

Wait too long and they'll shape themselves into a mob and tear you apart. But if you timed it just right, you could steal their will.

The secret was to pick a special man out of that circle, someone the whole camp looked down on. Someone who would crave respect like dope. You call that man over and when he comes — and he will, they always do — you've got the camp. They've missed their chance. They're ashamed for not standing up to you and you've given them someone else to loathe even more than they loathe themselves — your new toady.

In a few days the camp would empty itself. The men would move on. But for those few days, you're a king.

25 Rembrandt — 1932

IT WAS SELDOM HARD TO FIND a hobo camp. Each camp had a natural location. Always outside of town. Invariably downstream and in a hollow.

Town folk would tolerate a camp so long as the bums followed those rules. Being downstream meant the camp didn't dirty the town's water supply, and out of sight was out of mind.

Knowing the rules would get you close and once you were within a few hundred yards, the odour would come looking for you. Wood-smoke was the main ingredient with overtones of outdoor cooking and garbage. Which was which was a matter of frequent debate.

It was night as Rembrandt followed the men he'd travelled with down the wooded slope. This camp was all lean-tos and tents. No one here had bothered with building a shack. His group was approached by a man whose greasy beard and hair added their own ingredients to the camp scent.

"Report to the captain," he said, hitching a thumb over his shoulder.

The spot indicated was an open piece of ground where a group congregated around an open fire. On a stump sat a big one-eyed man. His one-eyed status was obvious. He didn't bother with a patch, just leaving the empty hole open to view.

Reporting at a hobo camp was new to Rembrandt, but having an adult tell him what to do wasn't. The other men muttered but shambled over with him. Whether by chance or design, when they got close to the one-eyed man, Rembrandt was in front.

"Empty your bindles and turn out your pockets." The greasy man had followed them and was giving more orders.

No one complied and the one-eyed man's gaze roamed over the group. The others kept quiet, waiting to see what would happen.

"Why?" asked Rembrandt, putting his neck in the noose.

"'Cause Slick Willy Palmer says so." One-Eye stood up slow.

How anything could seem funny just then, was a testament to how mixed up Rembrandt's head was. It had been less than a month since Uncle Thompson had died and that sadness had been a weight on him. But hearing that name, all he could think of were those happy days back at Three Farms chasing the dust devils. It brought a smile to his face and a load of trouble down on his head.

"What're you smilin' at, peckerhead?"

Slick Willy's big hands flexed in anticipation and the other men in the clearing sat up nervously.

"Just...dust devils, sir."

"Dust...? Why you little bastard!"

It wouldn't have mattered what Rembrandt said. Willy wanted to intimidate the new men and he'd picked the easiest target.

The first blow had an insolent quality to it. An open-handed slap, the sound cracked the night and knocked the boy to his knees. Blood gushed from his broken nose. Anyone could see it wasn't going to be a fight. It would be a beating, pure and simple.

And none of the other men interfered.

The boy was nothing to them — a stranger. Perhaps another day they might have spoken up, but Willy's craziness caught them unprepared.

The pain stunned Rembrandt, but it was the malice that rocked him. His folks had given him an occasional swat on the behind, but no adult at Three Farms ever struck him with anger in their heart. He looked up at two clenched fists.

"Why?" he gurgled through blooded lips. What had he done to this man?

Scarred knuckles struck and spun him like a rag-doll. He lay crumpled on the ground and thought the fight was over. But it wasn't.

"Now you're going to learn to watch your smart mouth, boy."

Rembrandt heard casual murder in that voice, like echoes of the clapboard church. Then, Pa had yelled "Run!", but now the boy could scarcely move. The one-eyed man was going to beat him to death. And no one was going to stop it. He was going to die just like Pa. He'd die...and the Devil would win.

Uncle Thompson had been so mad about losing Pa, so sure that he could've saved him if he'd been ready. So he'd drilled himself and young Rembrandt on those magic signs, until he was sure they both could make them, come hell or high water.

Rembrandt tried to think of what to do. He couldn't let the Black Bottle Man win. Everyone was depending on him. He had to do something.

Willy readied a kick as the boy rose shakily on hands and knees. The Texan's boots were pointed and metal tipped. Well suited to his purpose.

Snatching a hand to his broken nose, Rembrandt swept blood and phlegm across the dirt. He and Uncle Thompson had practised this sign plenty, just like all the rest, but they'd never added the spit or blood needed to make it change the world. It was one of the simplest signs to make and he made it good and big.

A single vertical line with four horizontal crossbars, like a busy telephone pole. The hobo sign for *police here*.

And the night erupted.

26 Rembrandt — 1932

FROM THE WOODS ABOVE came snarls and shouts, mixed from the throats of men and German shepherds. All around the hollow's edge dozens of headlights bloomed, strobing shadows everywhere. But this was no cavalry to the rescue.

The local sheriff's girl, caught coming home after curfew, swore she'd been chased by a hobo and her pa said, "I'll teach those thieving Bolsheviks a lesson."

Before you could say Jackie Robinson, every policeman from five counties was on those slopes, shotguns and pistols ready for business. And behind them came more armed men. A company of "bulls" — railway security police — the nemesis of the hobo. Someone thought they'd make good backup and invited them to the party.

The first gunshot was an accident. In the dark a root tripped a man, and *Bang*! no louder than a firecracker. The hollow held its breath a moment. Then the woods flashed like fireworks.

The voices of pistols and shotguns duelled to see who was loudest. No shadow was safe. Anything that moved was fair game.

It didn't last long. You can unload a gun into the dark faster than you can think. And there wasn't much thinking going on that night.

When it was over, the stink of cordite hung over the camp. The bulls and police were gone, taking their own dead and wounded, shot in the chaos.

The hobos had run. Some made it. Others not.

Morning looked in and found a boy sitting in the clearing near the dead fire. He was alone. His nose had stopped bleeding. But his heart felt like a bird in his chest.

"What have I done?"

27 Rembrandt —— 2007

THE SHARK BOYS WILL NEVER KNOW how close the Reaper came swinging.

Rembrandt had made the *police here* sign once in 1932 and innocent men had died. Tonight, a bit of spit and five lines on a windowpane could send five families to visit the morgue tomorrow.

That he will not do. But neither can he watch the street-woman become the object of the sharks' sadistic game.

So Rembrandt does not make the sign on the window. Instead, wetting a finger on an old pink tongue, he makes the five strokes on his own bare forearm. The police will come all right, but they will come for him.

If there is a price to be paid for invoking this sign, he will pay it himself. Back in '32 the hobo men might not have stood up to protect him from Slick Willy Palmer, but they hadn't deserved to die for it.

Having made the sign on his arm, Rembrandt expects something to happen but still the sudden whoop of a police car siren makes him jump. He ignores the sound of two car doors slamming. His eyes are on the shark boys.

Another ten seconds and they would've swarmed the street-woman. She is just too vulnerable for a shark to pass by. But the arrival of the black-and-white reshapes the sharks into young men of quality.

"Out for a stroll, thank you Officer."

And more importantly, it saves the young woman from harm. Except, Rembrandt sees, this does not seem to be so.

At the siren's whoop she turns and her hood falls back. Cleaned up the face would be pretty, if drawn. But her expression at seeing the police car is one of utter horror.

He turns too, expecting God knows what, but seeing only the two cops approaching him. Now behind him, the woman cries out in dismay and bolts into traffic, desperate to escape whatever it is she sees. A street symphony for horn and brake plays its disapproval, and she is gone.

He feels the bird in his chest again. Somehow he has caused this woman a terrible shock. The ghosts of men seventy years dead rebuke him.

"Don't you ever learn?"

28   Rembrandt — 2007

"KEEP YOUR HANDS WHERE WE CAN SEE 'EM, POPS."

The policemen, big men to start with, are bulked out with bullet-proof vests and equipment. They've not yet drawn their weapons but their right hands touch the butts of holstered guns like it wouldn't take much provocation.

Rembrandt does not reply. Instead he assumes a position most commonly seen on church crosses and on inner-city streets throughout the nation — arms outstretched, palms forward.

The policemen decide that isn't what they want. His hands are pulled behind his back and cold rings snicker around his wrists.

"Flashing the boys tonight are we, Pops?"

Rembrandt keeps silent. Hands flip open his coat, roughly checking belt and fly, dissatisfied by the lack of evidence. He is frog-marched to the curb and inserted into the back of the cruiser.

The back seat is vinyl, patched and repaired from a life spent accepting displaced anger. The car smells of human beings in all their wondrous variety, locked in a perpetual battle with cheap disinfectant. He is alone for a moment. The cops stand on the sidewalk looking around.

Witnesses with video cameras must make a cop's job difficult these days. Rembrandt wishes there'd been such things in 1932.

The handcuffs are hurtful things. Sharp metal edges make him grimace as he rubs at the skin-sign.

"Don't screw around back there, Pops."

The car springs creak and the cops take their places: driver and shotgun. Rembrandt leans back.

In the front seat there is a brief debate about how close it is to the end of shift and what they might do with the prisoner. No rights are read and Rembrandt does his best imitation of a harmless old man. He's a bit disappointed when they buy it. It seems he looks like a toothless old geezer, because that is what the man in the driver's seat calls him.

He is hauled back out of the black-and-white.

"We'll let you off with a warning, this time."

He "Yes-Sirs" and keeps his eyes on the ground. In his experience neither policemen nor gorillas like it when you look them in the eye. It must be that alpha-male thing that folks talked about so much a while back.

They drive away and he watches them go. The evening cool has come and he walks down to the Şally Ann where they've saved him a cot for his second night there.

Tomorrow he will go look for the street-woman and make what amends he can for what he has done to her.

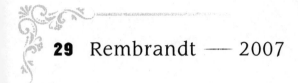

29 Rembrandt — 2007

NEXT MORNING REMBRANDT IS UP and out the door before the smell of coffee can rouse the rabble.

It has been another restless night. Between old memories and fresh guilt there's been a lot to think about.

He'd never seen the street-woman before, but as people sometimes do there is a quality about her that brings back long forgotten feelings.

Feelings for a girl who, if she is still alive, he hopes might remember him kindly.

AT AGE SIXTEEN REMBRANDT HAD BEEN on the road for five years, the last one all on his own.

Despite the loneliness he was never alone at meal-time. Careful use of *good fishin'* and similar signs kept him supplied with wild fish and game, always a popular addition to a hobo camp stew-pot.

He was careful never to catch too much. Uncle Thompson enjoyed how the miracle of the five trout made him a seven-day wonder, but since the violent night at Slick Willy's camp, Rembrandt had been cautious about overdoing the signs.

It was a hard life, but even the road couldn't stop a boy from growing. And with a growing body come new feelings. An ache that grows in your heart to find your someone, until it's like a wildfire roaring.

For Rembrandt the wildfire came riding on a plough horse.

He was walking north on a dusty Oklahoma road. It hadn't rained here for months and you could see the soil was dying. Every few miles another bank foreclosure sign was tacked to the front gate of a farm. It wouldn't be long before a lot more folks were homeless and on the move, looking for work.

Last night he'd decided to head back north. Texas was nice in the winter, but summer was coming, and with it the egg-frying heat.

The slow *clop-clop-clop* of hooves caught up with him first, then the horse drew beside him. It was dappled grey and old, a plough horse that had seen better days.

From the look in his liquid brown eyes you knew that the grey felt hard done by. That he should have been put out to pasture. But with the Depression and the drought, everyone had to work for their supper, even if it was just hay.

Perched bareback on this weary steed was a girl. Her yellow cotton dress flagged the sight of her tan legs clasping the old grey. Watching the way her calves gripped the flanks of that plough horse made Rembrandt stumble. She laughed and it was like cool well-water on a hot day. Rembrandt thought he would stumble all the way to North Dakota to hear that laugh again.

He found he couldn't stop looking at her. He had to see every part of her at once. His gaze leapt from raven hair, the gift of an Irish ancestor, to eyes as blue as cornflowers, to lips that made you dream of rose-petal kisses. From the cutest freckled nose to the... other parts that a respectful man wasn't supposed to be looking at.

But look he did. There was no helping it. He tried to look elsewhere, and discovered that that was where he was looking *again*.

It was like her bosoms were Magnetic North and he was a compass needle. He would have sworn that they were made perfect for the sole purpose of moving just that way, under a summer dress, while riding an old plough horse.

His face was red and he wanted to die from the embarrassment. By the time half of his wits caught up with them, there'd been introductions.

"I'm Leona, Leona Evans. My horse is Rocinante — Rocky for short. I named him out of a book, and I think Rembrandt is a nice name too."

He made an offer to walk her home and received an invitation to eat with her family.

"*If* my papa says it's all right."

Then they turned into a farmyard and a dog started to bark and some youngsters ran up to say "Hey!"

A woman, her momma, came out the screen door of the house, wiping her hands on an apron, "To shush that dog and see what all the commotion's about."

Leona slid off Rocky's back and disappeared from Rembrandt's sight for a moment. She reappeared, running with a small brown paper packet over to a farm truck, from under which sprouted a pair of trousered legs and sole-worn boots. She scooted under the truck, her bare legs next to the trousered ones.

Rembrandt heard how —

"Mr. Samson said no credit but took the trade goods you said to offer, Papa,"

And,

"That the part is used, but Mr. Samson says it's good-used."

And,

"Can I please, pretty please, invite someone to supper?"

Her momma, Mrs. Evans, took the grey's halter and looked at Rembrandt like she was judging between him and the plough horse, who would eat the most.

Then Leona and Leona's papa stood and they both joined in looking at Rembrandt too.

Mr. Evan's handshake was a wonder of communication. That one grip told Rembrandt two things:

— How the boy had better watch himself around Mr. Evan's daughter.

And,

— How these folks never turned away anyone from their table.

It was suddenly very important to Rembrandt to have this man's respect. So like Pa and Uncle Thompson was Leona's papa that the boy had to blink away watering eyes. He hoped his return grip gave a good account.

Leona took the handshake as approval and introduced the youngsters. Harvey, Lily, Sam Jr. and Ivy.

The way the four of them played tag around that horse's legs Rembrandt would've been hard pressed to say which was which, and from the look of long-tested tolerance on their mother's face it seemed that tag was a game without a beginning or an end.

Now that he looked more closely, Rembrandt could see how alike they were, mother and daughter. Remembering his manners, he offered Mrs. Evans his handshake. She took the offer but self-consciously hid her left hand behind her back.

Rembrandt guessed at what the trade goods might have been and felt sorry for the lady. For folks like these it would be shameful for a woman not to have her wedding ring. He hoped the part really was good-used.

"I have to mind supper." Mrs. Evans said, and went back into the house.

Soon the plough horse was in the barn and Rembrandt and Leona joined her papa under the truck like a pair of bookends, one on either side. Four varieties of "Tag, you're it!" kept them apprised of what the little ones were up to.

If he could've stayed under that truck for the rest of his life, Rembrandt would've died a happy man.

He wasn't much help with the repairs. Three Farms never owned a truck or a tractor but Mr. Evans showed him how things went together. And Leona's father liked to tease his daughter, so there were plenty more of those cool-water laughs Rembrandt liked so much.

He had to be careful where he looked though. Lying on her back like that and laughing brought out a whole new aspect to those bosoms, and to get caught looking by Mr. Evans seemed likely to be a firing-squad offence.

In between explanations of gaskets and lock-washers Mr. Evans's questions brought out the bones of Rembrandt's life story. He left out the Devil and the hobo signs, but at the telling of them leaving Three Farms and the loss of Pa and Uncle Thompson, Mr. Evans looked at him real close, like someone who'd heard a lot of hard luck stories and wasn't going to have his chain pulled by a liar.

He must have judged it the truth, if not the whole truth, because he offered his condolences on Rembrandt's losses.

"I'm sorry for your family too." Leona said. You could tell that she was thinking of the Evans' farm and how it would be to lose her own folks.

When the good-used part had taken its rightful place Mr. Evans taught Rembrandt how to work the truck's hand-crank starter without cracking his knuckles. A cloud of blue smoke announced success and Mr. Evans thanked Rembrandt, all formal, like it was him who'd done the repair.

Leona smiled at her papa for teasing Rembrandt too and the boy understood how one woman's face could've launched a thousand ships.

Her momma called, "Supper" once and there was no lolly-gagging around. Everyone was at the table before the screen door had time to slam shut. Rembrandt was placed on a bench between the two boys: Harvey, at ten the older boy on his left, and six-year-old Sam Jr. on his right.

Leona was opposite him, looking pleased as punch to have him there, with Lily and Ivy on either side of her. A great covered pot sent a good smelling steam into the air and it reminded Rembrandt of his ma's favourite Christmas story, by Mr. Dickens.

He saw the look Mr. Evans gave his wife, that silent communication between a couple who've shared hard times and happiness. The man's little nod at Rembrandt led to Mrs. Evans's asking —

"If our guest wouldn't please give the blessing."

It was Mr. Evans's way to show Leona's momma that he thought Rembrandt was okay. And it was a chance for the boy to prove it.

Rembrandt felt all hot and nervous, like he didn't even know what a blessing should sound like. Everyone shared hands with those next to them and bowed their heads. Harvey and Sam Jr.'s hands made Rembrandt welcome and he was able to speak.

"Dear Lord, we are thankful for Your blessings. Thank You for these kind folks who have welcomed me to sit at their table, as you welcome all to Yours. Thank You for the blessings of family and we ask that You keep all those who wander far from home in Your watchful care. Amen."

His own "Amen" caught him by surprise. Had the blessing been too short? Not thankful enough? He glanced over at Mrs. Evans, but she wasn't letting on what she thought.

Plates were passed and the big pot was emptied. It was a grain mash with some carrots and turnips for flavour. A postage stamp of pork fat might've been in there somewhere too. It was good stick-to-your-ribs food that would keep a farm family going.

Between spoonfuls Rembrandt took in the Evans' home. It took a hardpan determination to keep an Oklahoma house clean the way Leona's momma did, fighting the windblown dirt and what the feet of five children brought in the door. But if cleanliness was next to Godliness then Mrs. Evans deserved to sit at the Lord's table, right enough.

A much quieter form of the tag game continued under the table, as Harvey, Lily, Sam Jr. and Ivy surreptitiously kicked each other's shins. When one of them hit Leona and she returned the favour, her bare ankle touched Rembrandt's leg.

It was like a livewire had leapt up his body.

She must have felt it too, because she stopped eating and looked all flushed. That made Rembrandt blush all the more.

Luckily Mr. and Mrs. Evans were speaking to the little ones about minding their manners in front of a guest. They'd missed what Rembrandt felt sure was the sin of the century.

Supper was done and Rembrandt was sent outside with Mr. Evans and the little ones while Leona and her momma rattled up the dishes.

The setting sun promised a respite from the heat and the children switched from tag to hide-and-seek. The places you could hide in the barn and yard were well known to all, even little Ivy, so they were evenly matched.

When it was his turn to find the others, Harvey made a game out of coming close to Ivy's hiding place and singing a song about how,

"Mares eat oats,
And does eat oats,
And little lambs eat ivy,
A kid'll eat ivy too,
Wouldn't you?"

Each time Ivy got mad and came charging out of her hiding place, all set to tackle her older brother to the ground. Harvey let it happen and the other two children would join in the fracas.

Rembrandt and Mr. Evans talked about the weather and agreed a rain would sure be good. The way Mr. Evans asked about what the farms were like out west in California, Oregon and Washington you could hear his envy for all that good moisture.

There was no money to waste candles so when the sun set, bed linens were turned down. Rembrandt made to go, but somehow got sent to share the main floor back-bedroom with Harvey and Sam Jr.

The squeaky old iron bedstead was more swaybacked than the plough horse. Sam Jr. had the wall, Harvey took the valley in the middle and Rembrandt, as oldest was given the outside.

Lying in his long-johns Rembrandt could hear people in the two rooms overhead getting ready for sleep. He'd never strained his ears like he did that night.

It seemed the three girls had the giggles and the thought of Leona playing tag under the covers made Rembrandt sure that he was going straight to Hell, champion or no.

⊰⧉⊱

Next day he was up early, face washed and hair combed before Mrs. Evans came down to start breakfast. The crestfallen look on his face when he saw it was her on the stairs, instead of Leona, made Leona's momma laugh. It was a good laugh too. The laugh of a woman who knew that she'd been luckier than most, with five babies born and all of them living.

Rembrandt helped with the wood stove and hovered until she told him, "Get out of the kitchen and sit down, lan'sakes."

Soon others appeared: first the boys, then Ivy and Mr. Evans, and then Lily. But no Leona.

Her momma and papa exchanged another one of those looks and then at the sound of feet on the stairs Mr. Evans predicted, "Her Majesty's imminent arrival."

To Rembrandt, no fairy-tale princess could have been more beautiful. Her dress was the same yellow cotton one she'd worn yesterday but she had added a wide blue ribbon to her hair and her cheeks had a pink glow that put the prairie dawn to shame.

It didn't matter that the ribbon was from a First Prize button her papa had won years ago at the county fair, or that the pink glow came from pinching her cheeks a dozen times. She was more lovely than any world could hold for long.

In later years Rembrandt thought, maybe that was why folks had to get old and wrinkled. Being so perfect couldn't be allowed to last since we'd all been banished from The Garden.

Leona's papa warned Rembrandt, "You'd best close your mouth before you swallow a fly."

That made everyone laugh, the young ones for different reasons than their parents.

Breakfast was something flat and hot. Rembrandt didn't much notice. Magnetic North was getting stronger by the minute.

She'd been quiet at supper last night, but this morning Leona had found her voice. She chatted with her papa, not so strange after seeing them together yesterday. And she chatted with her momma, which put an expression of pure wonderment on Mrs. Evans's face.

She spoke airily to the young ones, like the gulf between sixteen and ten was wider than the sky.

Leona tried out some unfamiliar words from her *Don Quixote* book. They made her seem exotic to Rembrandt but brought on her momma's "wash your mouth out with soap" look. Not a word was spoken to Rembrandt, but every one was intended for his ears alone.

Then Leona's papa said, "This *soirée* is over, and would everyone please *sashay* out to the *cotillion*."

Mrs. Evans clamped her lips closed, trying hard not to laugh. She started snorting and had to get up from the table.

Turned loose, the little ones ran out the screen door to tag away another day.

Rembrandt's offer to help with the chores was well received by Mr. Evans and he followed Leona's papa out to the barn.

⁂

An empty house is a sad place, but an almost empty barn has its own lost air. The grey plough horse was the barn's sole occupant. Little hay and less grain remained to be parceled out.

It was a good barn. Rembrandt could see from the thick posts and beams that it was the product of a barn-raising. Neighbours had put their sweat and skill into this building and no doubt they'd had Mr. Evans's help in return.

Golden lines of morning sunlight striped the barn's barren stalls, and a half-haloed Mr. Evans asked for Rembrandt's assistance.

"I've a hundred things to do yet, to get the family ready," he said, "but I need to see Leona's old horse, Rocky here, sold. We wouldn't have kept him so long, but the girl loves the old creature so."

He patted the grey's wide flank and let his hand rest there, as much a sign of his affection for this animal as he could afford to show.

"It'd break Leona's heart to do it herself. I don't think she could. Would you please take the old boy into town and sell him for me and the family?"

Rembrandt listened respectfully and said he would, though the thought of doing anything that might hurt Leona took a bite out of him worse than the machine back in Tacoma.

"Thanks," Mr. Evans said. "The railway agent in town might give ten dollars for the old boy, but take eight, if offered."

It didn't seem right to ride Leona's horse, so Rembrandt led her friend — named out of a book — through the farmyard. Seeing him with the horse, the four youngsters stopped their commotion and that brought Mrs. Evans out the door.

Rembrandt realized that this woman had given up her own wedding ring before letting go of her daughter's horse.

He walked along, a hand on the grey's bridle, past the house. He saw Mrs. Evans turn to go back in, maybe to keep Leona busy for a minute, but it was too late.

The girl who had made his heart ache stepped out through the screen door smiling. Then she saw Rembrandt and the grey, and her smile dropped off the face of the Earth. He understood that she knew what was what. And he didn't stop.

THE WALK TO TOWN gave Rembrandt a piece of time to think. An old timer like Rocky wouldn't have much pull left in him, even if there was work that tractors hadn't taken over.

He figured that what Mr. Evans had asked him to do was to take Rocky on a walk down the last mile. The railway agent would be buying the horse for dog meat. It would be the last service Rocky could do for the family that loved him.

It would be hard for a man like Leona's papa to do that to an animal, a companion who'd given him so many years of help in the field. Rembrandt was sad to do it, but saw how it was a sign of acceptance by Mr. Evans. You wouldn't ask just anybody to take on this kind of a burden.

So when the railway agent was a jack-ass about the price, Rembrandt dickered like a Bedouin.

"Fiv' dallas." was the initial offer.

"Fit-teen." was the final. The agent paid it out in silver fifty-cent pieces.

Rembrandt showed Rocky the money so the horse could see how he was helping Leona's family this one last time. He thought he saw recognition in the big brown eyes.

"You do what you can for your family," they said.

Leona wasn't there, so he put his arms around the grey's neck for her.

To say goodbye.

32 Oklahoma — 1933

WALKING BACK TO THE EVANS' FARM, the silver made him feel like Judas Iscariot.

The day was gone when he knocked at the front porch post. The family was at the table, supper untouched. He opened the screen door and Leona left the room, headed upstairs.

He stood in the doorway, half in, half out, feeling unwelcome in a place and with people that had been more like a home and family than he'd known in far too long. Then Mrs. Evans wrapped her good momma arms around him and let him cry on her shoulder. She brought him inside and the children gathered around.

Little Ivy took his hand and told him, "It'll be all right tomorrow."

Mr. Evans thanked him, one man to another.

They had set a place for him at the table but despite the long day since breakfast he couldn't eat. He excused himself, put the silver in a cup in the cupboard, and went into the back bedroom to lie down.

The sounds from above were a just punishment. He listened just as hard this night as the last, but for a far different reason. He was ashamed for not being smart enough or rich enough to have a way to save this family from what the dustbowl was doing to them.

There were no theatrics going on above him. No spoiled girl, too-loud crying. Yesterday Leona had been dirt poor. Today, that was no different. But Rembrandt felt like he was worse than any Slick Willy Palmer. Willy hurt people and he meant to.

But Rembrandt knew now that he loved Leona. And that he had hurt her more than he could bear. Tears burned the back of his throat. After a long while he fell asleep.

Next morning at the Evans' farm, people moved about like folks do after a funeral. Mrs. Evans made stacks of pancakes, food being the all-purpose remedy to grief. And everyone ate. Even Leona.

Her papa had talked with her in the night about Rocky. And about Rembrandt. How it had been a kindness that Rembrandt had been doing for him. And for the family. And for her.

She learned that they had to leave Oklahoma. Papa thought maybe for California. And soon. That was why they'd needed the part for the truck so bad. And why Rocky had gone to town. He wouldn't be able to walk all those miles out west and none of the neighbours could take on another mouth to feed.

Papa told her how Rocky had done her proud. He'd thought the railway agent would pay eight or ten dollars for the old grey, but Rembrandt had brought back a full fifteen. That was some horse.

So between that and her momma rubbing her back and humming some lullabies, she'd passed away from feeling angry at Rembrandt.

Leona was a smart girl and, as is true of most young women, more mature than a young man like Rembrandt would be for many years. She'd seen right off how he liked her. Seen the red face and the goofy looks, and seen past them to the good young man he was.

They were people cast from the same metal, him and her. Not fancy like gold or silver, but something common, like brass. Long used in the world and stronger for being all mixed up.

She'd heard the troubles in his life, about his ma, pa and other kin, and her heart went out to him. It was the first hint of love and it felt green, and new, and right.

So all through breakfast Leona looked at Rembrandt. She was deciding. Deciding if she liked that face enough to look at it a good long while. The answer was yes.

She couldn't smile yet. But soon enough she would, and then he had better be ready.

⁂

Rembrandt hadn't thought of himself as slow-witted. But when he saw Mr. Evans breaking down the back bed that he'd shared with Harvey and Sam Jr. he got it. The truck part needed so badly. Mr. Evans's questions about California. The near-empty barn and Rocky's last mile.

The Evans family was picking up stakes. They were leaving Oklahoma. And...oh, Lord let it be possible! Maybe, they would let him come with them.

It might take them weeks, maybe months to find a place out west, and to a sixteen-year-old boy a few months seemed like forever.

Between the sadness over hurting Leona and the pure joy of this wondrous idea, Rembrandt scarcely knew what to do. He turned first to ask Mrs. Evans. She was boxing dishes in the kitchen.

But what if she said "no?" Mr. Evans wouldn't go against his wife's wishes.

Perhaps Mr. Evans? Rembrandt had helped with Rocky and all.

But Mr. Evans would see right through him. He was a man. He'd guess at Rembrandt's sinful yearnings for Leona. No. He couldn't ask Leona's papa.

Then Leona called him over to help carry a heavy box out to the truck and the problem was solved. She laid claim to him as her own and Rembrandt could feel how they all shifted to make a place for him in the family. A place where he belonged, just like the good-used part Leona had brought home and Mr. Evans had fit into the truck motor.

※※

With a house full of furniture and goods to load there was more than the truck could hold. So things had to be left behind. Some, like the chest of drawers that had belonged to Mrs. Evans's grandma, might've caused other folks to quarrel. But Leona's momma let it go without a qualm.

She said how, "The Israelites had left their grandma's dressers in Egypt, so I can't rightly complain."

Rembrandt saw Mr. Evans take one of the fancy brass handles off the chest when his wife wasn't looking and put it in his pocket. It would be a keepsake Leona's momma might enjoy having later.

Between the four of them, Leona, her momma and papa and Rembrandt, the truck was loaded by noon. The tires looked likely to pop and the goods were roped on that stake-bed truck like a boy-scout jamboree had stopped by to help. They wouldn't be going very fast and that would be just fine with one of the passengers.

Mr. Evans took the pilot's seat and Rembrandt had the honour of working the starter crank. As before, a cloud of blue smoke heralded success and everyone scrambled aboard.

Cubby-holes in back were lined with blankets and pillows for the little ones and the family dog. Mrs. Evans's place was in the cab, on the bench seat next to her husband.

Leona stood holding the passenger door open and Rembrandt knew it was for him. He slid in next to Mrs. Evans and Leona followed, closing the truck door.

It was a tight fit with the four of them in the cab together, and Rembrandt had to squeeze his eyes shut on account of Leona's leg being pressed up against his and no place to go. They would be riding like that for hours and days.

And this time the bird in his chest felt happy and good.

MR. AND MRS. EVANS WERE SMART FOLKS but they hadn't been on the road the way Rembrandt had. It made him feel proud how they consulted with him on what route to take and where to stop. He hadn't seen the Oklahoma panhandle before but experience in the hobo world was valuable anywhere.

Back in their own community the Evans family were known and respected. But ten miles down the road they were strangers and the locals would be suspicious.

The boy could've led them to the hobo camps along the way. But you didn't have to be a genius to see all the ways that would lead to trouble. So he steered the family away from many a place that would've left them shipwrecked on the plains. They might not know it, but Rembrandt did and that was plenty.

His remarkable prowess as a fisherman raised Mr. Evans's eyebrows so many times it became a family joke.

"All Mr. Evans has to do," Leona's momma said, "is wrinkle his brow and 'poof!' there Rembrandt is with a big fat trout, or pike, or catfish."

It's funny how folks will do that. See something and turn it around, all backwards. Like the pre-Christian pagans who thought Jupiter or Thor made thunder and lightning, when it was hearing the boom and seeing the flash that caused those folks to create little gods in their heads and start believing in them. Young Rembrandt thought people sure were foolish in the old days.

The fish and game he caught along the way made more of a difference than any of them knew. The Evans family was part of the earliest wave of Okies to head west. Many then and later would see their children starve. Not just go hungry, but starve — to death. And that in a country with plenty of food to spare.

Except for buying gas and oil for the truck, they were able to avoid the towns along the way. Since they would move on each morning, Rembrandt found them spots to camp upstream of the towns. Gone after a night, the townsfolk never had time to even know that they were there.

He grew to be a part of their family. Harvey and Sam Jr. took to hitching up their pants just the way Rembrandt did. He made wooden dolls, one each for Lily and Ivy and used a few drops of cooking oil to bring out the grain, so the dolls seemed to be wearing fancy clothes like the ladies in India. Of course the best part of life was being with Leona every day.

Mrs. Evans said, "Rembrandt's filling out to be a fine figure of a man."

The rail-thin boy was growing taller by the day and new muscles made his shirt tight across the chest. He could tell Leona liked that. Sometimes he thought that a bit of Magnetic North might be rubbing off on him.

The two of them were seldom alone for long though. Leona's folks liked Rembrandt plenty, but still they had to look out for their daughter. More than one love-struck Oklahoma girl had allowed the stirrings of womanhood to whip up a batch of motherhood.

For Leona and Rembrandt, sitting up tight against each other in the truck cab each day was like rubbing two sticks together. You can't do that for long before you start a fire.

34 Colorado — 1933

"THE EVANS FAMILY TRAVELLING ROAD SHOW," as Mr. Evans called it, had been following a jig-jog path west-by-north-west for three weeks the day that one of the truck tires blew, just on the other side of Sugar City, Colorado.

There were many worse places in the world it could have happened. The sight of a pretty little lake ringed by green fields and cupped by mountains made you forget about dust storms and dying crops.

Jacking up the overloaded truck on a mountain road was a hairy job, but Mr. Evans and Rembrandt scavenged up a couple of deadfalls to brace the wheels and they had the flat tire off in good time.

Mr. Evans went to see about having it patched in Sugar City. If he was back in time they could keep going that day. If not, there was a pine grove nearby, where they could camp for the night and head out in the morning.

Also near the truck was a patch of what Ivy dubbed "coneflowers." Leona and the girls used them to weave princess crowns for themselves and their mother.

Mrs. Evans looked uncomfortable during the coronation, and then blushed for the first time since he'd known her when Rembrandt swept a grand bow from sky to ground and called her, "My Queen." Leona laughed with the rest but went after Rembrandt with an angry-pixie look in her eyes.

"My Queen, hey?"

She got her fingers into his ribs and he fell down from the tickling, taking her with him. Then he started in on tickling her too and the two of them were tickling each other, giggling and crying "Stop! Stop!" and "You stop first!"

They ended up tangled in the flowers, with Leona on top. Rembrandt's palms held her up by the rib cage, fingers digging for more giggles. Leona must have been filling out too, because her bosoms seemed about ready to pop out of that old yellow cotton dress.

The tickling stopped. Their eyes locked and Magnetic North had two poles that day.

Leona leaned toward him, taking a million years until their lips were so close every breath was sweet with the taste of her. Rembrandt waited.

He forgot that Mrs. Evans and the little ones could see them, and wouldn't have cared even if he hadn't.

Gentler than an opening blossom, Leona's lips met his. So soft and warm, as light as spring dew, they swept away all that he'd ever imagined a kiss could be. Then, each lingering, not wanting to part, she lifted her head up again. The sight of her eyes filled his.

"I love you," he said.

From down the road a man's voice whooped a, "Whooo-hoe!" The joyful cry shot past them all and echoed back from the mountains. Rembrandt and Leona sat up out of the flowers, their happiness glowing. Leona's momma and the children were looking east, toward the town. Coming up the road was Mr. Evans, running toward them, waving his arms.

"Whooo-hoe!" came the cry again.

First Mrs. Evans, then Ivy and then everyone was running down the mountain road toward him.

With a third whoop Mr. Evans grabbed up his wife and spun the two of them around. In a moment that echoed in Rembrandt's heart, the man and woman tumbled to the ground, her above and him below.

"Have you lost your mind, Mr. Evans?" Leona's momma had to smooth down her skirts.

Mr. Evans grabbed her and succeeded in planting a great smacking kiss on her lips. The children were talking all at once.

"What is it, Papa?"

"Are you okay, Momma?"

"Where's the tire, Papa? Did it get lost?"

"Papa kissed Momma just like Leona kissed Rembrandt."

That one must have caught Mr. Evans's attention because he helped his wife up and dusted off his trousers seat in jig time. Rembrandt felt his face getting red.

Then Leona's little, warm hand took his, showing everyone how things stood. The pixie look was back in her eye and Rembrandt felt taller than ever.

"I love him, Papa," she said.

Then it was Mrs. Evans's turn to remind her husband to close *his* mouth before *he* swallowed a fly. Leona's parents looked at Rembrandt and he realized the next line was his.

"Uh, Mr. Evans, I do too. I mean, I love Leona too."

Leona hugged his arm. Her bosoms pressed against his bicep and the fire feelings started to grow again.

The children were giggling and imitating Rembrandt's pronouncement of love in the deepest voices they could manage. Leona's momma shushed them and turned to look for Mr. Evans's response.

All fathers need to practice for this moment and clearly Mr. Evans was as unprepared for it as Rembrandt had been. Poor men.

"Uh, I got a job." That was what Mr. Evans said.

"What?" Mrs. Evans said.

"Down in Sugar City."

"What? Where?"

"Sugar City, like I sa—"

"I know that, where in Sugar City?"

"The sugar beet plant—"

"What sugar beet plant?"

"The one in Sugar City."

They could have gone on like this for quite a while but Mr. Evans held up a hand for quiet and got five sentences out in a row.

"I was at the garage in Sugar City. There was a notice about them needing a mechanic at the sugar beet plant. While the tire was being repaired I went over. They hired me. And the pay is enough for us to — "

Or at least, four and a half sentences. Mrs. Evans was the one doing the kissing this time. Leona followed her momma's good example and planted one on Rembrandt that made the planet change orbit.

When the grown-ups had finished kissing and "harrumphed" enough to get the young couple to finish as well, they started talking about what to do next.

The tire-shop man arrived and helped the men get the truck back together. A three-point turn and they were headed the mile east into Sugar City, Colorado, population two-hundred fifty.

From the back came the voices of Harvey and Sam Jr. remarking at the buildings and the cars. Lily and Ivy called out "Hey," to the ladies and children they passed and waved to everyone like they were in a parade.

The sugar beet plant was big and gave off lots of steam. That impressed everyone and Mr. Evans hoped out loud that he could help Rembrandt find work there too.

They stopped by the plant manager's home and got directions to a house they could room at until they found their own place. Mr. Evans said that with the regular hours and pay he thought they might look for a little farm. That would help with the groceries and give them a new start. Mrs. Evans said the same things, only more so and kept looking at Leona and Rembrandt with a happy, and a sad kind of smile.

Leona kept whispering "I love you, Rembrandt" in his ear, and hugged his arm, too excited to stop. The only one who was quiet was Rembrandt.

He had thought this time was a long way off. They weren't even a quarter of the way to California. It should have been months before...

He couldn't even about think it.

35 Colorado — 1933

REMBRANDT TRIED VERY HARD not to think about the twelve-day time limit that had ruled his life.

After a few days at the boarding house, he helped Mr. Evans find a farm place the family could take on a rent-to-own arrangement. That put off the inevitable a short while, but each tomorrow came no matter how hard Rembrandt wished for it to wait.

After moving into the new house, Mr. Evans had a man-to-man talk with him about Leona. It was awkward and when it was over, neither was sure which of them was the more embarrassed. It was about how Leona's papa had come to like the young man. How he didn't want either one of the two young people getting hurt. And he hoped that Rembrandt would give it a good long think and ... well, if he wanted to ask for Leona's hand in marriage, he would have Mr. and Mrs. Evans's blessing.

It was what Rembrandt wanted more than anything in his young life. He loved Leona and knew she loved him back. He thought he would make her a good husband. And he hated the Devil with a passion few mortal men could match.

The next morning he told Leona the truth.

They started out sitting close on the porch glider that had come with the new farmhouse. Now she was pulled back to one side of the bench, shaking her head at a most peculiar story.

"Your papa sold your soul to the Devil?"

Leona had enough of her momma in her that it was going to take a second time through to clarify everything.

"No, I still have my soul. It's just wagered you might say. Along with Pa's and Uncle Thompson's. If I can find a champion—"

"To beat the Devil?"

"Yes, then our souls, and Aunt Annie and Aunt Emma's souls, can all go to Heaven when we die."

"And until you find the...?"

"Champion. Yes, I can't stay longer than twelve days in any one place."

"'Cause if you do, the Devil kills you?"

"Or he gets people to do it, like the church-folk that killed Pa and whoever it was that killed Uncle Thompson when he was in the hospital in Montana."

"And you can do magic...?"

"The hobo signs at first and now the skin signs, yes."

"Magic."

Leona was looking at him like she thought he was drunk.

"Look, I'll show you. After Uncle Thompson died, there was some trouble at a hobo camp. I didn't kill them, but some men died because I made a sign for the police to come. A man was going to kill me you see—"

"The Black Bottle Man?"

"No, that's a different man. This was Slick Willy Palmer and he was just a crazy man."

"A crazy man." Leona's voice was full of uncertainty.

"Anyway, after the men died at the camp I thought, 'What if I could have gotten away from Slick Willy?' Then no one would have gotten hurt. You see?"

"O — kay..."

"So, that's what I did. It took a long time, but I invented a sign so no one can see me."

Rembrandt pulled back the sleeve of his shirt and held out his forearm. With a quick lick of his finger he drew a *don't see me* sign on his arm and Leona let out a shriek, the like to take paint off a barn.

"Rembrandt!"

He wiped off the mark and she hugged him hard.

"Rembrandt!"

The front door opened and Leona's momma stepped out onto the porch.

"Y'all right, honey?"

Leona released her beau and let out a breath. "Yes, Momma. I'm fine."

Mrs. Evans waited a minute to see if there was more, then went back inside to finish what she'd been doing.

"I'm scared Rembrandt."

"Me too."

"What can we do?"

"I don't know. Find a champion to beat the Devil, I guess."

⚜

He looked. He looked hard. And when the twelve days were up he left the Evans' new farm.

Leona, like most girls, thought her folks wouldn't understand and so she and Rembrandt pretended that it was something the young couple had decided on themselves.

"It's not right," she told her parents, "For a girl's intended to be sleeping at her house. Rembrandt will just find another farm to stay at, and come to call until the time is right for a wedding."

Their new neighbours were willing to put him up so long as he helped out. And the next neighbours, and the next. But Sugar City wasn't a prairie town, with places in every direction. It was a community strung along a single road through a mountain valley. There was the town proper, which under the Pact, counted as one place, and then there were the farms every mile or so along the road.

Pretty soon, between using up the places that would take him and those that didn't want or need someone staying there overnight, Rembrandt had to walk farther and farther, just to see Leona for an hour or two each day.

Folks started to talk about the odd young man who wouldn't stay put for more than a dozen days at a time; Leona's folks started to lose their trust in Rembrandt. And still no champion.

"You've got to find one, Rembrandt."

"I'm trying!"

"I can come with you."

The day had come when all the places along that road for miles and miles had been used up. Rembrandt's options had run out. He loved Leona more than ever but knew he couldn't do that to her. He couldn't take her on the road.

Pa had known it and left Ma behind. Uncle Thompson had known it and refused to inflict the hurt of love-lost on Mrs. Arlington back in Tacoma.

He blamed himself for not seeing it. For loving Leona and hurting her with that love.

"No. You can't come."

"I will. You can't stop me."

"Leona..."

"I will. I'll follow you."

"I'll come back. I'll find the champion and I'll come back."

And in his young heart Rembrandt was sure he would, or die trying.

36 Gail — 2007

ALL MUSIC CONTAINS WITHIN ITSELF a kind of divine madness.

Few will read a book or watch the same film more than once, but everyone returns to their favourite songs. Of all the arts, music is the king of repeated experience.

Raymond, whose fascination with the American Civil War always remained part of the male mystery to Gail, told her a story about how, during Sherman's siege of Atlanta, the fighting would pause each evening while in the trenches a rebel soldier played "I Dreamt I Dwelt in Marble Halls" on his brass cornet. Both sides would hold their fire, each man clinging to those few moments of beauty to diminish another day's loss of friends and comrades.

For many of those men, despite the melody's association with death and pain, it was a piece of music they felt compelled to return to time and again, for the rest of their lives.

Since the shooting, Gail has chosen a number of self-imposed punishments. Gathering broken glass, the morning count of "3-5-9," and leaving home and husband to live alone on the streets.

She's never explained this to anyone, and there is one punishment that she's kept most secret. It's a vow. Not of silence. But to forsake music.

William Congreve, British playwright and grave-mate to the great composer Handel once wrote, "Music has charms to soothe a savage breast." But Gail does not wish her heart's pain to be pacified.

Sin calls for penance. And she has sinned greatly. No one else knows how greatly.

On that final, fragile day, after the last bell rang to end classes, Gail had kept her students late. From the classroom CD-player came a piece of music as unfamiliar to the children as it was intimately known to Gail.

On her desk stood a tall mahogany pyramid — a newly-won metronome. It was handmade and Italian, more trophy than practical instrument, and on its front a small gold plaque proclaimed:

> Classical Composition — 2006
> Second Prize
> Gail Brewer for "Illuminating"

❧

"How briefly lasts the crowning green of glory?" the Italian poet Dante Alheghieri had asked.

❧

The children were in their seats, listening when the man she came to know as Andrew Franklin Moore opened the door. She thought he might be a parent, drawn in by the melody. It pleased her inordinately to share "Illuminating" with another adult.

❧

Of the seven deadly sins — Superbia — Latin for Pride, is the original and most deadly. It is Lucifer's own, most personal sin. It is the *why* and the *what* of his existence: why he rebelled against God, what he most understands, and why the Proud are his favourite projects.

Gail cannot carry stone slabs upon her back like the proud sinners of Dante's *Inferno*, but she means to bear this penance until God is satisfied.

Where, you might ask, in a modern city, can you go where you will not encounter music? Better yet to ask, "Where, in your own head can you go, where you will not hear it?"

How can anyone forsake melody, harmony and rhythm, and remain human? How does one renounce pitch, volume, timbre and resonance, and still stay sane? But Gail will not relent. She does not tap her toe, nor sing or hum or whistle. And she most certainly will never compose again.

Her "crowning green of glory" lasted a single day.

"Nothing but a gust of wind," as Dante said.

BY AGE NINETEEN, Rembrandt had spent three years training one man after another to fight the Devil. Like an addicted gambler, as soon as he had scraped together another bet, there he was again, rolling the bones against the Black Bottle Man.

You might think it would be hard to find volunteers for such a crazy business. But you'd be wrong. There were plenty of men, so confident in their own righteousness, he could have charged a hundred dollars a head. Each man was convinced their faith was flawless. That they would be the one to place their boot on the Devil's neck.

There got to be a pattern to it. He told his story. The hobo signs proved he wasn't crazy and then the fellow would talk himself into it. Rembrandt could hardly get past "You'll fight the Devil himself" and they were sold — lock, stock and barrel.

He taught each man the signs he'd invented by then, but The Pact must have imposed some kind of caveat. Because aside from himself, Uncle Thompson, and Pa, no other person could make them work until they'd sworn to fight the Devil.

Once the commitment was made, they could do the magic. Until then, they could learn the shapes, try spit or blood or tears, and nothing would happen. But once they'd placed their bet, they were magic. And they all loved it.

The man would start talking like he was Merlin, or Moses, maybe the Second Coming. It made Rembrandt sick, but Leona was waiting. So he turned a blind eye. He let himself believe that if the man failed, that he would learn from that failure and do better next time.

In those three short years, six champions called the Devil.

Each time, before the Black Bottle Man came, a kind of unplanned ritual took place. Rembrandt didn't want it, but each time, the man insisted on talking about his "destiny."

It got the young man thinking about his Uncle Billy and how he'd joined up for the Great War before Rembrandt was born. Billy had enlisted, thinking he would be the one to capture the Kaiser. He told young Rembrandt, "Those who didn't put away such foolish ideas didn't survive long at the front."

You see it's not the generals and politicians who lead men to their deaths. It's King Arthur and Lancelot. It's the stories that fathers tell sons. Stories of triumphant heroes. Tales repeated until we believe them.

In the 1940's the newspapers said in Germany a man called Goebbels had invented something called "The Big Lie." But that too was a lie. Goebbels invented nothing. Homer had beaten him to it by twenty-five hundred years.

Every man Rembrandt recruited to fight the Devil thought he was a hero — a person of *destiny*. It made Rembrandt realize how, in our own stories, aren't we each the hero?

It was that understanding that stopped him. Did he think that he was a hero? Would a hero use these men so? Firing them into the dark, the way the cops back at Slick Willy's camp had shot at shadows — spending bullets without a thought to what they might cost others?

What he was doing was worse than the Great War generals. These men weren't his cannon-fodder. They were his hell-fodder.

And Leona. She waited for years. He wrote when he could, saying that he would be in a certain town around a certain date and she would write him back. At first her letters were long and full of news about her momma and papa and the little ones.

Birthdays and holidays came and went and Leona and Rembrandt poured out their love for each other into those letters. But with all that pouring, and so little to replenish it, love gets used up.

"X"s on a piece of paper were no substitute for the kisses they'd given each other. Love denied its proper life, gets twisted up and hurts the lovers.

So in the end, Rembrandt let her go. After a final letter to Leona, he stopped looking for champions and went looking to find his ma.

"REMBRANDT!"

It was his ma. Greyer and more careworn, but still his ma. Their embrace was clumsy. Her arms remembered the boy of ten and were unprepared for the man of nineteen. Had she always been so tiny?

"Oh, Rembrandt. You're home!"

There was no heart in him for saying "No" to his ma. Not after all the loss and failure.

"Father, it's Rembrandt!"

A stooped, balding man stood nearby. His collar starched and his clothes well brushed. This was his front parlour and it matched the man. Spotless and well-ordered, no sentimental brick-a-brack cluttering the tables. None of Rembrandt's mother's things were anywhere to be seen. The stooped man, his grandfather, did not approach.

"Get him cleaned up." An ebony cane stamped new marks into the dark wood floor as the old man left the room. Ma did not try to call him back.

"I'm sorry Rembrandt. That's just the way Father is."

"Ma...." He needed to tell her about Uncle Thompson. He hadn't written.

"Come to the kitchen. You must be famished."

In that moment Rembrandt felt the absence of Pa and Uncle Thompson more keenly than he had in years. They'd walked away from Three Farms together, the three musketeers. More damned storybook heroes. How could he be here, and they not? The taste of failure was scaly and rough in his mouth.

His ma led him down a dark hall to the kitchen. He looked back at the footprints his boots had left behind them. Grandpa was right—he was dirty.

Ma sliced bread and opened three kinds of jam. She put on a kettle for tea and poured him a big glass of milk. It was like she wanted to keep his mouth full so that the bad news couldn't come out.

Rembrandt could sense emotions at war within his ma. Hope battled fear. He knew that when he told her everything, the casualties would be terrible. Then, having let her feed him half a loaf of bread with jam, chased down by a quart of milk, Rembrandt stood up and stopped her bustling.

"Ma."

Her arms found their new place around his chest. Her head lay against his breastbone and he held her, kissing the top of her sweet head.

"Ma, Uncle Thompson…"

"I know, I know."

"He died in Montana. In '32"

"Oh, Rembrandt! No!"

She understood of course. When Rembrandt had come to the door alone, unannounced, Ma had first looked at him. But she had also looked past him, searching for Thompson. Not finding her brother-in-law, she must have steeled herself for that loss. But hearing that her boy had been alone and on the road at the age of fifteen, with both his pa and uncle dead, that was a blow that she had not prepared for.

"I meant to write…"

"I got the letter about your pa from…"

"Mrs. Arlington."

"Yes."

Ma raised his right hand and studied his arm in wonder. "These skin signs? They're safe? Not like what Annie and Emma did?"

Rembrandt shrugged, uncertain. "I think so. Uncle Thompson thought so. And Pa, maybe."

"It's God's own miracle. Oh, and now you're safe home again."

"Ma—" He didn't want to have to say it so soon.

She was shaking her head, trying not to listen.

"Ma...I tried. I did."

"No."

"The men I found, who tried to fight—"

"No, Rembrandt!"

"It isn't over, Ma. I'm sorry."

She shrank and folded down onto the floor like her flesh was melting wax. "I prayed every night..."

"I'm so sorry, Ma." Rembrandt knelt and took her hand.

Then she traded her bad news for his. "They're here, Rembrandt."

The tone of her voice left no question who "they" were. The women who'd lived in the south house. His aunts, Annie and Emma.

"And their babies, grown now. Both girls. Almost nine."

Rembrandt felt strange and distant, like the part inside that was him had walked to the far corner of his head.

"Your cousins, Germaine and Bridget."

"Why here?"

A voice from the dark hallway broke through. "Because our own families sent us away."

It was Pa's sister, his Aunt Annie standing in the doorway. He helped his mother to her feet.

As with their parting, there was no embrace from Aunt Annie. Echoes of Pa's and Uncle Thompson's faces in hers were an affront to him. She was so little aged and now he saw – with a heart changed by his love for Leona – how Uncle Billy must have seen her.

Why Uncle Billy had fallen back to drinking when the Black Bottle Man's promise made everything go so wrong for them. Rembrandt had felt the call of the whiskey bottle himself these past three years. As a boy he'd judged Billy, condemning the man's weakness. Now that was tempered with empathy for someone tested past his strength. Rembrandt felt past his own.

"The return of the prodigal son." Aunt Annie smirked.

Ma's eyes narrowed. It seemed that Aunt Annie had made some poor joke at his expense. He did not give her the satisfaction of asking what she meant.

Another woman spoke. "You're the image of your pa." It was Aunt Emma. She was there too, standing in the shadowed hallway behind Annie. Neither woman entered the kitchen. Rembrandt sensed some invisible line, some unspoken agreement, kept them out of Ma's kitchen, a place where they'd once been so welcome.

"A little on the grubby side though, wouldn't you say?" Annie wrinkled her nose and his ma spoke up.

"Ladies. Please allow me my time with my son." Rembrandt had never heard Ma so possessive.

"Of course," Emma agreed.

Annie said, "Your cousin Bridget will be home from school soon. You'll want to meet her, Rembrandt. And Emma's Germaine too I suppose."

"What do you mean by—" Emma started but Ma closed the kitchen door on the rebuke.

"Your grandfather is a stern man, Rembrandt. But he agreed to take those women and their babies in when no one else would or could. Times are…" She stopped.

His ma must have realized how foolish saying "times are hard" would sound to a young man who'd lived so many years hand-to-mouth on the road.

"Are the girls…?" Rembrandt hardly knew what to ask.

"Bridget and Germaine are normal enough, considering how their mothers are. I try very hard to remember that none of this is their fault. Come."

His mother led him up the back stairs, what the servants would have used, before the Depression and five extra mouths had strained her father's resources to the limit.

To Rembrandt the second floor held the wonders of Xanadu. There was indoor plumbing, cold and hot running water and a bathtub. He was embarrassed that Ma had to show him how it all worked.

"There's plenty of soap. I'll see if I can find some of your pa's clothes that might fit."

Of course she'd brought all of Pa's things back east with her. They'd all hoped it would be over quickly. He locked the bathroom door, tried to scrub the stink off and thought about Aunt Annie's too delicate nose.

39 Montreal — 1937

"GIRLS, THIS IS MY SON, your cousin Rembrandt."

Rembrandt stood in his pa's best shirt and trousers, newly ironed and smelling of hot mothballs.

This third floor room had been given over to the two girl cousins. Evidently his Grandpa didn't much like to climb stairs because the order of the parlour was not repeated here. Here was the happy chaos of childhood. It was Rembrandt's favourite room in the whole house.

At the moment it was crowded. He, Ma, the two aunts and the two girls stood among art easels and tables covered with books and toys.

"Hello girls," he said.

The two of them looked at him with big, curious eyes. Their physical resemblance was strong. Having the same father would have a lot to do with that.

Aunt Annie stood next to her daughter, Bridget, challenging Rembrandt's right to even look at the girl. But he crouched down like Uncle Thompson had, the day The Pact was made, and tried to see Bridget the way Ma suggested, as an innocent.

Her hair was brown, grown long, but tightly braided and pinned. It must have hurt to get those braids so taut. Bridget looked more used to indoors than out, and her generous smile made him feel each of the hardscrabble years he'd spent on the road. All those years he'd missed knowing this little cousin.

"Hello, Cousin Rembrandt." She said it like she was greeting royalty.

The formality here made Rembrandt feel foreign. Even the way Ma spoke now had been changed by coming back east.

A poke from Aunt Annie prompted a pinafore'd curtsy. He thought that Bridget's mother must have heard stories of her own, about common girls rising above their station.

"Hello, Bridget. Is that Germaine?"

The second girl, on the other side of the room, peeked from behind her mother, Emma. Very much like her cousin in colouring, Germaine's long hair was unbound. Bridget took his hand and led him over to meet Auntie Emma and Germaine.

Emma's expression was quite different from Annie's. Now that no one stood between them Rembrandt saw Emma's eyes glistening with grief. As he neared, her chin began to tremble as she fought to be stoic.

"Oh, Rembrandt," Emma crumbled. "I'm so sorry!"

Rembrandt folded his arms over her shoulders, holding his aunt like an unknown danger.

"Oh, Thompson! Thompson, I'm so sorry!" Emma's sobs came in deep shuttering breaths.

With Pa gone, eleven-year-old Rembrandt had become Uncle Thompson's sounding board. That was how he'd learned so much about the Black Bottle and the instruction letter. And how Rembrandt knew, that despite her betrayal, despite her fall into sin, Uncle Thompson had never stopped loving this woman.

Snapping footsteps and a slammed door signaled Annie's departure. Bridget had been left behind, to make what she would of all this on her own.

Germaine clung to her weeping mother's hip. Then the girl flung out an arm to include Rembrandt in her embrace. Her sympathetic wail played counterpoint to Emma's murmured apologies.

Bridget stood nearby, unsure what to do. Rembrandt looked to his ma. She shook her head, denying involvement in any part of this. She remained rooted to her place near the door. He felt how strained this household must be. No wonder his grandfather was unhappy to see another of the unsettled prairie folk in his house. Half a day here and Rembrandt already felt older.

Emma's need for absolution blazed like a pyre in the room. Of anyone, Rembrandt felt least capable of giving that gift, but Ma's rectitude was plain. She had given too much to her sister-in-law already. A husband and a son cast into the fire was plenty. For Emma to ask for unearned forgiveness was intolerable.

What will you think of me, Ma? Rembrandt wondered. I've been weak too.

She was right though. Emma hadn't done anything to deserve his forgiveness, not yet. Perhaps that might come later. Perhaps not. He couldn't find it in himself to absolve her. But for the sake of the little girl, he could try to comfort her mother.

"Aunt Emma, Uncle Thompson always loved you." That at least was not a lie.

Rembrandt touched Germaine's head, asking her to look at him. "And Germaine I know your pa would have been so proud of you."

He was talking about Uncle Thompson, not Billy. He'd walked many roads with Thompson and believed he had some measure of the man. No question, Uncle Thompson would have loved this little girl with all his heart. It made him smile to think of what mischief Thompson would have gotten into with a child of his own, and he shared that smile with her now.

"He was a great man, your pa. I know he would have loved you, Germaine."

He saw her quietly repeat those words, "He would have loved you Germaine," so that they would always be true. Germaine buried her head in the folds of Pa's old shirt. Emma nodded her thanks and wiped her tear-washed face.

"Did you know my poppa too, Cousin Rembrandt?" Bridget asked.

"Yes, I did Bridget."

Uncle Billy had faltered, but he was a man like any other. Like me, Rembrandt thought. I have no right to cast that first stone. But how can I explain that to her?

"I haven't seen Uncle Billy in a good while, but I know he always loved your ma, very much."

"Did he love me, Cousin Rembrandt?"

Rembrandt looked to his ma again for help. He didn't know if they had seen anything of Uncle Billy since the man left Three Farms. But Ma withheld herself again and a small stone formed in his heart. Even here he was alone.

"I never got a chance to ask him, but a fine girl like you, I'm sure would have been the apple of his eye."

Bridget took his one hand while Germaine captured the other. It was clear they wanted to know all about their fathers and wouldn't be letting him go until he'd told all the stories he could remember of the days on Three Farms and the happy times on the road with Uncle Thompson.

Aunt Emma and Ma left, pulling the door closed behind them. Rembrandt heard his ma say, "You stay out of there Annie."

The door stayed closed. No one entered, but Rembrandt felt his aunt's presence nonetheless.

A bell rang from downstairs.

"Come on Rembrandt, suppertime."

The girl cousins were out the door and down the stairs. It reminded Rembrandt of Lily and Ivy running to their momma's call of "Supper!" Though it hurt, he welcomed the remembrance. Memories of Leona and her family were slipping away. The loss felt like God's judgment upon him for the things he'd done since leaving Sugar City.

The door stood open and Aunt Annie barred his way.

"Who the hell do you think you are?" She demanded. He could practically smell the fumes coming off of her.

"I never asked your pa. I never asked Thompson. And I certainly never asked a snot-nosed ten-year-old boy to interfere in my business. What the hell did you think you were doing?"

"I—"

"I made my choice. Get that? My. Choice."

"Uh —?"

"You don't think it was worth it? Bridget's everything I could have hoped for, smart, talented, beautiful."

"Aunt—"

"Billy couldn't give me a child, so I made it happen myself. I knew the price. My soul for my baby. Don't you think your oh-so-perfect mama would have done the same for you?"

The stairs creaked and Aunt Emma appeared.

"Annie what are—" Emma began.

Now Annie turned on her. "You're sorry! You're sorry! Well, I'm not sorry. I've got Bridget."

"I wasn't—" Rembrandt said.

Annie's ire returned to lash him.

"Don't you understand, Rembrandt? I knew the Black Bottle Man would come. I knew I was selling my soul so my daughter would live. There was no need for your pa or Thompson or you to be oh-so noble and save me. I knew what would happen. And I chose!"

Emma looked down the stairs and tried to give warning. "Annie, don't—"

But Annie was beyond warning.

"So don't you come around here, filling Bridget's head with sentimental notions about how wonderful her pa was. He was a drunkard when I met him. I wasted my life on him. And he was a drunkard when I left him."

Another figure was on the stairs. It was Bridget. The girl's face drained white but still she delivered her message. "Supper..." Then she fled.

Rembrandt pushed past the aunts. Annie flailed at him, wanting to hurt him. But her notion of violence was something from a fairy-tale book. It barely slowed him and a trail of alarmed faces led him down the stairs.

Germaine at the second floor landing. His grandfather on the main floor. Ma in the dining room waiting for everyone to come to supper. The porch door stood open and the front gate's clash proved Bridget's passage. Rembrandt's long legs sped him after her.

On the sidewalk leading south, a bobby pin lay where it had been thrown. Ahead, the figure of a girl half-ran, hands grasping at her hair, pulling at pins and braids like a hateful thing was on her head. Rembrandt followed at a distance and waited.

Standing on the sidewalk, unmindful of the passing neighbours, Bridget raked each braid apart and littered the ground with the detestable pins.

"A drunkard!" Her voice was liquid, full of pain. "When we met! When I left him! A drunkard!"

No one else from the house had followed. Not one.

Rembrandt went to her, and started to kick and stomp those hair pins. His boots sent them flying. She joined in and they held hands to keep each other's balance.

"Crummy," he started them off.

"Rotten," she joined in.

"Stupid."

"Stinking!"

"Useless!"

"Pins!"

When it was over, both were out of breath and Bridget might have learned a hobo cuss word or two.

"Cousin Rembrandt?" she asked. "Can you stay with us forever?"

⚜

For ten months he was able to remain close enough to visit Bridget and Germaine.

He'd thought he was coming to Montreal to see his ma. After all the defeats, all he'd wanted to do was to hide his face in his mother's skirts and cry.

But what he'd found here was a gift — the gift of these two girls, these two Black Bottle babies.

There were more hard words from Aunt Annie. He saw how she hated the guilt she carried over the sacrifice her brothers had made for her. He thought about how Pa and Thompson could've loved their sister so much, and yet not understood her. And how she could love them so much still, that hating them was easier than grieving for them.

The last thing he said to Annie before he left might not have been fair, but he felt it was true.

"Annie, you're right," he said. "Bridget was worth the price you paid."

PORCHES ARE MEANT for goodbyes.

When the time came for Rembrandt to leave Montreal, everyone was there, gathered on the veranda of his grandfather's house. Ma hovered, on the verge of tears. Aunt Emma, brave with a boxed lunch bursting with baking and treats, food once again the stand-in for feelings. Germaine in command of his suitcase, the first Rembrandt had ever owned, now filled with Pa's best clothes, her mouth set firm like she meant to march away down the road with him. Bridget beamed at him with the pride and fellowship only the luckiest of cousins can share.

Aunt Annie — merely present.

It was his grandfather's parting gift that surprised Rembrandt the most.

"Here." The old man pressed a thin wad of papers into the boy's hand. On top were four American one-dollar bills, a grub-stake that would get him off to a good start.

"I found them in an old suit pocket," his grandfather said.

The money was clipped to a red cardboard certificate, as intricately engraved as any bank note. It announced that,

> This Ticket entitles the bearer to
> Second Class Passage
> from Montreal, Que. to Boston, Mass. — Return
> The Boston, Concord and Montreal Railroad

Creases around the old gentleman's eyes deepened and for a moment they were two knights-errant, *en passant*.

"You're a good boy, son," the elder said, and Rembrandt wished that were more true.

Ma safety-pinned the ticket and the money inside his hand-me-down coat and straightened his pocket-handkerchief, like that would fix everything.

"I've a friend in Boston," Grandpa explained. "Laurence Ginsberg. Grew up just down the street. Sounds strange to say, but Larry's a Jewish Bible scholar, smart as a whip. I've written his name and address on the back of the ticket. Tell him about The Pact. Show him your signs. Maybe he can help."

A glint of moisture visited the old man's eyes and Rembrandt glanced away. He didn't promise to come back. He'd learned that much at least.

41 Rembrandt — New Hampshire — 1938

FINDING UNCLE BILLY was never part of the plan.

❧

After all the boxcar years, Grandpa's second-class ticket was like a pass through Alice's looking glass.

The train seats, set in pairs facing each other, two fore, two aft, provided their own definition of proper human posture and at each stop Rembrandt's car gained and lost a few passengers, each assisted by a white-jacketed porter who patrolled the aisle, dubbing all men "Sir" in the hope of garnering another nickel.

There was nothing fancy about the other passengers. Many were travelling salesmen, their sample cases on display in the overhead compartment or tucked under their seat. This one pushed brushes, that one hawked musical instruments.

Once aboard, some of the men tugged fedoras down over their eyes, glad for even the half-sleep you could steal from a straight-backed train seat. Unfolded wings of newspaper allowed others to ignore their neighbours and the world around them and substitute someone else's words for their own wisdom.

The train took him south, across the American border into territory Rembrandt hadn't seen before. First Vermont, where the lingering smell of maple syrup made his mouth water for Ma's waffles and pancakes. Then New Hampshire, a strong, granite-backed country, with mountains and forests scabbed with logging camps, where under other circumstances he might have stopped, looking for work.

Maybe his grandfather's friend would have the answer. Tomorrow might be a very different day. Rembrandt pretended to be carefree and gave the passing vistas his full attention. Sometime after they'd passed through Crawford Notch, Rembrandt looked up to find that someone new had taken the seat opposite him.

The man's face was hidden behind a copy of *The Saturday Evening Post*. A Norman Rockwell illustration graced the cover, and an ad for Chesterfield cigarettes on the back paid for it. Wedged under the man's seat, between boots set wide apart, was a tight wooden crate. Stencilled on the side were the words, "*Fragile — Glass.*"

Those words were a fish-hook and they caught Rembrandt, mouth agape.

The boots and trousers, black. Frock coat, black and clean. Arms bulged with muscle, bigger than Rembrandt remembered. Nails like whole cashews, thick and striated, tipped long fingers that held the *Post* in a greasy grip.

"You!" Rembrandt remembered his hands ablaze with pins and needles and the stench of an elm tree's corrupted heartwood.

The magazine wall fell and a frog-lipped mouth smiled *hello*. It was the Black Bottle Man.

Whether the surprise on the Black Bottle Man's face was real or feigned, Rembrandt could not have said. If real, if this encounter was unplanned, then this would be what the generals called a "meeting engagement," when enemy forces collide by chance and the upper hand goes to the first to seize the initiative. Rembrandt meant for that to be him.

A square of strong noon sunlight warmed both their knees as the train followed the curve of a mountain's shoulder. For Rembrandt the terrain shifted more acutely than it did for his fellow passengers. Then inspiration struck. The time to act was now.

He raised his hands, surprised to find them steady and beckoned the larger man like a pugilist, to come and take him on.

"Me. You'll fight me." Rembrandt said.

There was a new-found confidence in his voice. The tone of someone certain they've suddenly discovered the secret key to success. The Black Bottle Man examined his challenger and shook his head, producing a sound like dried rattlesnake tails.

"No," he said.

"Why? Why not?" Rembrandt was impatient, demanding his rights. "That's the answer. I should be my own champion."

"Are you stupid, boy?" The Black Bottle Man lingered over the insult.

"It's true. I've got you figured." The words were coming fast now. Thoughts half-formed, to be spoken before the thread was lost. "That's how you beat people. Making them rely on others, when they should rely on themselves. That's the trick in The Pact."

"No, it ain't."

"My pa could've beat you."

"No, he couldn't."

"Or Uncle Thompson, if he'd tried."

"Nope, not him neither."

"Damn you!"

That produced a piece of flint in the old demon's eyes.

"Already been done, son."

"Fight me!" Rembrandt's balled fists shook.

"Listen boy. You're tapped. You've got nothin' left to bet with."

"I've got—"

"You've got nothing. Your soul is already in the pot."

"But—"

"Nothing to wager means you're no champion. And don't go thinking you'll get someone else to put up their soul so you can fight." With his two middle fingers the Black Bottle Man stroked a worn spot on the breast of his coat, to the left of where his heart should be. "I've got The Pact right here."

The touch was too intimate for a public place and Rembrandt felt soiled by the sight.

"I know it well. One of my favourites. Got plenty of spice." The pale tip of the man's tongue poked out from between the frog-lips, like an earthworm trying to escape, and for a long second he rested the too intimate fingertips on it.

"Yummy."

His hand slipped inside the frock coat and extracted one of the pages missing from Ma's family Bible. The text of *Leviticus* held the center of the sheet like an infantry square, but a more important story was told in the margin notes. Around the edges in rust-tinged ink wound the Devil's copperplate hand, like a legal Ouroboros, a worm of words seeking to swallow itself.

"See here." The Black Bottle Man turned the page upside-down to find the passage. "'Each champion must agree that their soul will go into the pot too.' *Ergo ipso facto*, no pitch-hitting."

Rembrandt was stymied, speechless. He felt robbed. It had made perfect sense. If you wanted something done, do it yourself. But now his legs had been kicked out from under him. The train slowed, huffing to a stop. A town had slipped up alongside. The sign said: *North Conway, New Hampshire.*

The station was a long, low building with taller end blocks that looked like a pair of lady librarians startled from their studies.

The Black Bottle Man rose from his seat, dismissing the boy. He smacked his copy of the *Post* with the back of his hand and hurled it to the floor, a gauntlet to someone else's challenge.

"They think a made-up magazine story can keep 'Mr. Scratch' out of New Hampshire?" His voice carried a tone of rebuke The Furies might have envied. "Daniel Webster. We'll see."

He dragged out his wooden box and calming, cradled it, cooing. At the compartment door he stopped and with a new semblance of surprise called back to Rembrandt. "Why not keep it in the family?" He pointed at a man working at the south end of the platform. "I'm sure he'd love to take a crack at me."

Rembrandt leaned out the window to look and the thrill of recognition touched his heart. There, loading a bundle into the back of a round-hipped Ford pick-up truck was a man he hadn't seen in half a lifetime. Not since that awful morning in Ma's summer kitchen, forever ago, in a life that lay on the other side of Pa and Thompson's deaths like a foreign land, glimpsed only briefly through eyes too young to understand. His Uncle Billy.

"I've got other business here," the Black Bottle Man interrupted. Then he spoke so only the softest pieces of his voice reached the boy. "Call me when he's ready."

Taller, slimmer now, a new stranger in town, the Black Bottle Man climbed down the train-car steps, crossed the platform and headed north, up the street toward the Court House.

Rembrandt found himself on the platform too, suitcase in hand. The station was a hive of activity. On his left, from the first-class cars, streamed well-dressed men and women, boys and girls. Some carried short leather riding crops, many were dressed in jodhpurs and riding jackets, like a British fox hunt gone astray. Down the line on his right, where the box cars trailed the passenger cars, workmen hooked wooden ramps in place and dozens of fine thoroughbred horses were led down onto the turf by handlers and stable-boys. Cries of "Momma! Poppa!", "You there, porter!", "Careful with that!" filled the air with an insistence easily associated with those who remained rich in a time of want.

A friendly little man with a compact Leica camera moved through the crowd, snapping candid pictures, capturing this happy horse-back invasion of North Conway for *Life* magazine. The sudden tumult filled the space between Rembrandt and Billy.

"Uncle Billy!" Rembrandt's call was lost amidst the general chaos. It never would have occurred to him to stay on the train.

"Uncle Billy!" The young man moved, pushing through the crowd, at cross purposes to the equestrian stream.

A grin hit his face like a punch. Pa and Thompson had been the more important men in his life, but there was no denying the pull of family. He'd known Billy every day of the first ten years of his life. Now, like an opened treasure box, all the valued memories of this man came flooding back.

The crowd was gone and thoughts of the past departed.

Suspenders made a wide detour around the contours of Uncle Billy's stomach. The man had a great deal more belly than Rembrandt remembered but if the stains on his porkpie hat were any indication he was still a hard worker, not afraid of honest sweat.

Confusion and hope swept Billy's face, in parts more comical than a Charlie Chaplin film.

"Who...?" Billy cocked his head, a hound uncertain of a fading scent.

"It's me, Billy. Rembrandt."

The older man's jaw dropped and he barked a laugh that carried the smell of cheap whisky. "Rembrandt! Little Rembrandt?"

"Grown some."

Lost comrades, the two men embraced and for now the Black Bottle Man's intimidations were forgotten.

"Come on." Billy's parcel was shoved further into the Ford's box and the tailgate closed with linchpins dropped into place. "This calls for a toast."

He waved his nephew into the passenger seat. In the truck's rear window a wooden rack cradled a rifle, stock to the driver's side, barrel to the passenger's. Rembrandt slid in, past the muzzle. A partly-used box of shells, a testament to the weapon's frequent use, adorned the dashboard. The lingering smell said that the truck cab was Billy's favourite hunting spot.

Not since the day they'd gone to claim the wooden box from Montreal had the two of them ridden together like this, and the moment did not pass unnoticed. Billy stomped the floor starter button and the Ford rattled to life; no hand crank in need of an eager boy. Then they were away, headed east, the train and station falling away behind them, a torn-up mountain-side ahead.

At first Rembrandt thought it must be a strip mine, an open pit cut into the mountain to extract coal or similar. Then his uncle clarified the sight.

"Ski runs." Billy tilted his chin at the mountain. "Where I work. My boss Mr. Gibson's goin' to make the biggest winter resort in the world. Got a German ski expert. Was run out of Austria."

A flat glass pint bottle made a brief but energetic visit to Billy's lips and then was passed over to Rembrandt. The black and white label said *Lincoln Inn Old Rye Whiskey, 100 Proof.* It too had come here from Montreal.

"You're a man now. Have a nip."

Rembrandt complied, accepting the film of spit that coated the bottle's warm mouth. At fifty percent alcohol, the rye hit his gullet like a carpenter's rasp.

Billy was all questions. "How'd you find me?" And "How are your folks?"

The real question of — "Does Annie want me to come back?" — hung between them, but Rembrandt had far more important information to relate.

He had told a version of this story exactly six times before. Once to each chosen champion. Six times between Sugar City and Montreal. But those men were strangers, who didn't know the people. Billy did. And in his way, had loved them. And abandoned them.

Rembrandt pulled no punches. There was no gentle way to explain that Billy had run from the real fight before he even knew what was at stake.

Each new revelation landed another a blow. His uncle reeled and pulled off the road, hands loose on the wheel. The Ford was left to find its own way into an alpine meadow, crunching gravel to a stop. Rembrandt switched off the motor, and the engine block ticked an irregular time. In the distance, bulldozers and drag lines stripped the mountain's dignity for the sake of winter tourist dollars.

It took more than an hour to tell it all. The whisky bottle, its contents long forgotten, was smeared with Billy's palm-prints, wrung hard, like his hands longed to wring his own neck.

The demonstration of the hobo signs seemed like an anti-climax with Billy. After the first, the older man hauled out his shirt-tails and showed Rembrandt a brief glimpse of his belly, where the markings Annie and Emma had inked into his skin that moonless night nine years before, still lay inscribed, as strange as any skin-sign the younger man had yet invented. The idea of skin-signs was no surprise to him.

"Jesus. Two girls?"

"Mhmmm." Rembrandt mumbled the answer. After his time in Montreal he could hardly confirm it. In his heart, Germaine truly was Thompson's daughter, no matter the facts.

"My turn now, eh?" Billy said. It wasn't really a question.

"Yes." Rembrandt had briefly thought about not telling Billy the truth; of spinning out some yarn about everyone still living happily at Three Farms. But he'd carried the weight of this burden alone for so long. To have someone who would truly understand was too much of a temptation to resist.

To have someone motivated not by self-righteous pride, but by love of family, that was a friendly shore to a shipwrecked man.

The Black Bottle Man had pointed him at this island, and he had to assume that the Prince of Lies had his own purposes, but how could he have walked away?

The sense of relief, of turning over responsibility to someone older and wiser flooded his mind. Billy had been to war. He'd seen the elephant. If anyone knew how to fight, it would be him.

⚜

"You've got to practise, Billy."

They'd gone to where his uncle had bed and board. Thrown up to accommodate the influx of rough-necks working on the new ski resort, the place had more in common with a hobo camp than a rooming house. A ramshackle affair of wooden additions smothered the original house, which crouched somewhere inside. Men's shirts and underwear hung on lines strung from the windows, flapping a threadbare semaphore that signaled who knew what. A breeze skirted the house and left smelling strongly of Boston baked beans, both before and after consumption.

Rembrandt's suitcase was unpacked into a chest of drawers handed down from nobody's grandma and seeing how thin his uncle's wardrobe was, Rembrandt proposed that they share and share-alike. Who needed more than two shirts anyway?

Down to business, Billy accepted the terms of the Pact without a second thought. Rembrandt had barely shown him the basics and already the man was impatient.

"How'd the other champions do?" Billy wanted to know. "These ones do 'em any good?"

"Well... Yeah. Some." Rembrandt didn't like the implication. "Pa and Thompson figured the signs were God's way of helping us out."

Billy grunted at that one. "You can make new ones, that right?"

Rembrandt nodded.

"Me too? I can make new ones if I want, right?"

"I guess so." Rembrandt didn't know. None of the other champions had ever tried.

"It's not that easy Uncle Billy." Perfecting the *don't see me* had taken him months of trial and error. "And some are real dangerous."

"Leave this to me," Billy said. "I see more skin-signs in the outhouse every morning than you've had hot dinners. I know as much about 'em as anybody."

"But, there's not a lot of time." Billy wasn't listening. "If you don't call the Devil within twelve days, he'll come looking for you. You've got to let me teach—"

"I'll be back, soon as I've got the answer." Billy scooped clothes from one of the newly filled drawers back into Rembrandt's bag. "I'll just borrow this for a few days. You stay here."

⚜

Billy was back, mid-afternoon on a Sunday. It was the eighth day since Rembrandt had arrived in New Hampshire. The older man stood in the rooming house door, Pa's shirttails out, no luggage.

"I've got him now," he said, proud as a bantam rooster.

"You'd better show me," Rembrandt said. His mouth was cotton dry. But Billy wanted to keep his secret to himself.

"Come on," he said, tilting his pork-pied head. "Surprise is worth a battalion."

Outside, the Ford was running. Billy climbed into the cab and Rembrandt had no choice but to join him.

"And I've got a couple up my sleeve." Billy snorted off a laugh. Then he got serious.

"We'll fight on the ground of my choosing," he said. This was followed by the profound statement that, "The best defence is a good offence." and Rembrandt knew that "destiny" had taken hold of his uncle. He glanced over, not sure whether Robert E. Lee or Napoleon Bonaparte was in the driver's seat.

Billy soon wheeled them into a deserted construction yard. The sign said, *Cranmore Mountain Resort*. A chain link fence surrounded a graveled square, materials and equipment crammed together like Fibber McGee's closet. Empty barrels rubbed tarry shoulders with forklifts. A mountain of lumber threatened wooden avalanches and the guts of a steam-shovel lay spilled on the ground, repairs left for Monday morning.

Billy stopped the truck next to a rack filled with lead pipe and announced, "This is the place."

He must have already called the Devil, because Rembrandt could see the Black Bottle Man across the yard, leaning against the steel-cleated track of a bulldozer. The old demon gave the machine an affectionate pat and shrugged out of his coat. It was a gesture so human, yet for Rembrandt it was freighted with significance. Never before, against any champion, had the Black Bottle Man removed his spotless coat.

Billy dropped his left arm below the dashboard, out of sight and stripped back his sleeve, sharing a sneak preview with Rembrandt. His forearm was red and raw from days of abuse. A new tattoo crossed from outside wrist to inside elbow like a remembrance of trench warfare. Two jagged lines, a doubled thunderbolt, had been permanently inked into his skin.

"Just watch me." His voice had claws, wild for revenge. Then the truck cab door flew open and Billy was a blur of motion, faster than Rembrandt would've believed possible.

He was a cobra. No, he was lightning. His fists whip-cracked like bullets and the Black Bottle Man was instantly staggered, knocked to his knees. Billy was right. He had the element of surprise.

A light filled Billy's face and he declaimed as though he were Achilles at the gates of Troy, "It *is* sweeter far than flowing honey.'"

Billy let his adversary climb to his feet. The worm-tongue tasted blood on fist-stung lips.

"This is more like it, boy." The Black Bottle Man addressed himself to Rembrandt with a tone of mild pleasure, like someone who has sampled an improved recipe and two of the three men knew that the fight was over.

Billy wasn't one of them. He hadn't seen the Black Bottle Man, back at Three Farms, the day he snatched Ma's family Bible out of the air, snake fast.

Now both men blurred. Fist met fist and mortal flesh failed. Teeth flew like shrapnel and Rembrandt flinched. A broken incisor flensed his cheek. Billy was on the ground, jaw out of kilter, neck broken. Another dead hero to join the Stygian host.

The Great Serpent roared a challenge at Heaven. "Bruise my head will they?"

The time to be silent passed and Rembrandt spoke.

"Why don't you just kill me too?"

"Oh no, my boy." The reply came as the Devil went. "I wish I had six more just like you."

42 Rembrandt — 1938

THE SKY WAS OVERCAST in North Conway, New Hampshire. The air heavy with the promise of an ocean-born storm.

Rembrandt buried his Uncle Billy on a hillside above the town, surrounded by headstones older than he could imagine. 1670. 1680. Despite the age of these markers the spirits of the dead seemed close. He was not alone on this Cemetery Hill.

Beyond a reef of tombstones two families huddled under a cloud of unneeded umbrellas. Raised against the threat of rain, once up, some silent code said it would be disrespectful to lower them again. In the centre of their circle, the slim casket that connected them waited to be added to the Earth.

A man, not much older than Rembrandt himself, held the hand of a little boy. A grandmother stood close, cradling a baby. There was no young mother to be seen. No need to guess where she must be.

Rembrandt waited respectfully. He and Billy were in no rush and North Conway was not their town.

Rituals were observed and words were said. An old hymn was sung. Voices broke and fell away and by the fourth verse Rembrandt could only hear the young husband, bravely promising that —

When for a while we part,
This thought will soothe our pain,

That we shall still be joined in heart,
And one day meet again.

Rembrandt wasn't there to see his pa buried. Nor Uncle Thompson. He didn't even know where their last remains lay. So when these folks were done he would take his time, honoring his dead with extra prayers.

The other people soon drifted away in twos and threes. A grandfather took the little boy down the hill, back home. An older woman visited another, smaller gravestone. Some earlier loss.

The young husband remained as grey day became night. The clouds shredded to let the moon hold vigil and Rembrandt did right by Billy. Across the valley the White Mountains shone, promising to be good company.

Rembrandt did not speak to the other man. Nothing was said about the Pact or skin-signs. He didn't tell anyone about them again for a very long time.

43 Boston — 1938

BOSTON WAS A SHAMBLES.

While Rembrandt had been at the boarding-house in North Conway waiting for Uncle Billy, Mother Nature had laid a harsh hand upon the North-Eastern Seaboard.

In late September 1938, when the autumn equinox tide was at its highest, what would come to be known as The Great Hurricane had found New England unprepared.

First striking the smallest state with the longest name — Rhode Island and Providence Plantations — the storm surge, strengthened by the harmonic tide, topped the high water mark by thirteen feet and sped inland. Spread two hundred miles wide, it inundated not only the coasts of Rhode Island but those of Connecticut and Massachusetts as well.

Hundreds died. Hundreds more went missing.

In Boston, Professor Ginsberg's hillside neighborhood stood above the storm surge's reach but had traded floodwater for wind. Now many of the houses on that hill were piles of rubble. The few not flattened were crippled and maimed, eyeless victims of hundred-mile-an-hour gusts.

Tilted and rhomboid, the Ginsberg home waited quietly for Rembrandt. This day carried the chill of a Labrador low, but no smoke rose from the remaining stump of a chimney. Instead, an iodine smell recalled to Rembrandt that bad leap-year Sunday on the Pacific North-West, and he feared he'd come too late.

With the flooding and disrupted roads and railways it had taken him weeks to reach Boston, then days more to find the address his grandfather had written on the back of the train ticket. By now there should have been people here, repairing and rebuilding. But there were none.

He stood on a patch of dry sidewalk across the street, amid the chaos of uprooted trees. Trunks and boughs lay like Bridget's hairpins, scattered where the storm had kicked them.

Though it still stood, the roofs and walls of the Professor's home were canted at unwholesome angles. Rembrandt crossed the road and climbed the front steps, then stopped and surveyed the street. On a piece of broken fence a thinning cat waited with feigned indifference for its master's return. The front door to the house, half-unhinged, hung down like a torn lip.

"Hello? Is anyone home?" Rembrandt was not surprised when his calls went unanswered.

He scraped mud from his boots and stepped over the threshold. Hopeful that the Professor would forgive him his trespasses, he hung his hat and coat in the oak and leaded-glass vestibule and moved on. The scent of pipe tobacco lingered and a colony of books owned the front parlor.

Ostensibly the Ginsberg's parlor had been a compromise, with the front half, nearest the bay windows being reserved for the reception of guests, while the back half had been surrendered for the Professor's study. But the steady creep of books and papers across settees and chairs into the social spaces revealed the irresistible power of a scholar at work.

Meaning to leave a note, Rembrandt opened a walnut roll-top desk. Inside a dozen cubbyholes were stuffed with letters that sported stamps from dry, foreign places. Despite the spreading clutter elsewhere, the work surface of the desk was remarkably spare. On the right, a china cup and saucer in a yellow-budgie pattern sat, dried empty, the tannin film skinning the inside surface of the cup.

Rembrandt imagined the scene. A man is ready to enjoy a cup of tea when his solid house groans. He drops the desk's roll-top to keep his papers safe and goes out to close the storm shutters, thinking that will be enough. The tea cools, and over days, evaporates, untasted.

To the left lay a baked tablet of tan clay, dimpled with tiny triangles, like a spray of miniature hobo signs. Where it was from or how old it might be Rembrandt could not have guessed, but its air of antiquity was unassailable and he did not presume to touch such a treasure. Next to it was what he'd sought. A pencil and a writing pad.

But he paused. On the pad, in a careful hand was the Professor's unfinished work, a translation of the markings on the clay tablet. Curious, he read the notes aloud:

Lugalbanda (3rd Sumerian king of Uruk, father of Gilgamesh, 2700 B.C.?)
he has ventured into the faraway places /
no mother to offer advice /
no father to talk to him /
no one is with him whom he knows, whom he values, no confidant is there to talk to him/

His own life's parallels to this ancient prologue left Rembrandt unsettled and suddenly the room felt like a tomb he must not disturb. Rembrandt returned the note pad to its rightful place and closed the desk, trying not to think of coffin lids. He had no proof, but did not doubt that Laurence Ginsberg was dead.

Who knew what he might have learned from the man? What had his stop in North Conway cost him? But had he been here, would the storm have taken his life too?

Had the Black Bottle Man saved him, or had the old demon stopped him from finding a way to win?

Rembrandt left the house and walked away. Forty-seven hundred years ago a Sumerian king had travelled a path similar to his, perhaps on a similar quest.

He left Boston to mend its own wounds, certain after seeing the clay tablet that the hobo signs were far more ancient and far more important that he'd ever imagined.

44 Rembrandt — 2007

EVERY LIFE HAS A TEMPO. Farmers match the pace of the seasons, just as fishermen bend their wills to accommodate the tides. The city inhales office workers at nine and exhales them at five. And within a city's main beat there are counterpoints. The nightshift that keeps rhythm until the day-shifters return; and the outsiders, the homeless, their lives are a jazz riff that plays around the theme.

Old Rembrandt follows that riff seeking to find the street-woman. Unknown at the shelters and soup kitchens, it becomes obvious that she must be haunting the furthest fringe. So that is where he looks.

He is too old to be skulking through the dark crannies of a city, so instead he uses the best ally an old man can have. Patience.

In an area abandoned by city planners and ignored by all but the dregs, he finds a comfortable place to sit, unobserved. And then he waits for something to happen.

The day passes and evening is collecting shadows to build another night, when a car that does not belong drives past and stops. It is twenty years old but clean and well cared for. The kind of car an older, practical woman might own.

Curious, he shifts from his vantage and shuffles closer. There is no need for stealth. Another old bum will attract no attention here. He fits into the landscape.

Then his gut twists as the occupants of the car pull black balaclava masks down over their heads. It's another hot summer night. No one would wear masks in this heat.

Rembrandt looks around, wondering if the Black Bottle Man is near. If these two are hunting the street-woman, it's no wonder she's frightened.

A quick *don't see me* lets him trail the hunters. But how strange? One, he can tell is a man, maybe thirty. But the other moves like an older woman. And she is carrying a white box, like you might be given for leftovers at a nice restaurant. Did Meals-on-Wheels wear masks now? Then a snippet of their conversation puts an end to his concerns.

"It's a good stew, Louise," the man says.

"Do you think Gail's safe here, Raymond?"

"No, but... I don't know what to do anymore."

Rembrandt drops back. It's clear they aren't intent on doing mischief and eavesdropping is rude. He won't use the sign magic just to be nosy. The man and woman turn a corner and he follows at a distance.

They find a shadowed stairwell and the woman sets the food box down in a fading pool of light. They back away. Timid hands grow out of the shadows and take the box, withdrawing into the darkness. The man and woman retreat and speak again as they pass the un-seen Rembrandt.

"She's okay Louise." The man pulls off his mask, rubbing his sweaty face. He is clean cut with a sadness that lives around his eyes.

"Do you think so?" The woman, also unmasked, reveals an older version of the street-woman — her mother? She dares a quick look back.

"Yes...."

Then they are gone.

The stew does smell good. Rembrandt sits on the stairwell, holding onto the *don't see me*, watching the street-woman — Gail? — eat.

The smell makes his stomach growl and the woman stops. There are dogs and worse that might interrupt your meal in a place like this. Rembrandt fears hers is a life soon destined for a meaningless end. Much like his own.

Dozens of empty food boxes lie scattered about. It seems Gail receives daily deliveries from Raymond and Louise. It's good to see that someone cares for her.

Then, sitting on those concrete steps Rembrandt allows himself to accept it. The time for champions is over. He will never find anyone who can beat the Devil. It's been a fool's errand chosen by his father. The sins of the father, paid for by the son.

"Oh, Pa." The lament escapes.

"Who's there?" The street-woman asks. Her tone is warm and gentle, not afraid. Maybe invisible ghosts or whispering shadows are safer for her than cops.

"My name is Rembrandt," he replies. "Is it all right if I just sit here a while?"

She seems to like being asked.

"Of course, Mr. Rembrandt." Then like a memory of kindergarten she offers to share. "Would you like some stew?"

"Yes. Thank you, Miss."

"Oh, you can call me Gail."

She holds out the remains of the boxed stew and Rembrandt accepts the kindness. She smiles, and he thinks how rare a thing it must be for her now, the chance to give to another. Even a humble gift brings honour to the giver.

Yes, there will be no champion now, but Rembrandt thinks about the giving of honour. The time he has left is short but there is someone in his life he would very much like to honour, his angel of mercy, Mrs. Arlington. He'd always loved Mrs. Arlington for what she'd done for him — giving him the time he needed to tell the story of Pa's death in his own words.

And he can see that for this young woman — Gail — her life might soon be over. There are people who care about her — Raymond and Louise. But he'd heard no words pass between them and Gail. He thinks how Raymond and Louise might treasure a letter from their lost one.

He lets the *don't see me* go. She seems okay with that. And from a pocket he produces a pencil stub and some paper.

"Gail, I know that there are folks who love you. I'm ready to write down whatever you have to say to them. Okay?"

She looks at him a long time. Then she swallows and says, "Okay."

45 Rembrandt & Gail —— 2007

WHEN YOU'VE BEEN LOOKING for something for a very long time, there's always that moment, when you see it, when you can't quite believe it. For Rembrandt, it is like that with Gail.

He'd thought that it was him doing a kindness for Gail, to sit with her and write down the words that her hands could not touch. But this evening with her has been a blessing to him as well.

Always on the move, always hoping for a champion who could beat the Devil —that had stolen from him the simple pleasure of caring about someone else's needs. With Gail, he is given the chance to just listen. Like the way Mrs. Arlington had listened to him all those years ago in Tacoma.

He'd been trying to be the Great Teacher for so long, that he'd forgotten how to be anything else.

Gail's story reminds him of the price to be paid for following the Lord's direction to turn the other cheek. The day Andrew Franklin Moore invaded her classroom, Gail's only chance to protect those children had been to surrender all hope of resistance and to empathize with that man. She'd drawn all of Moore's attention and all of his wrath down upon herself to defend those innocents, even though it meant losing herself.

It could not have been plainer. Gail is Rembrandt's last, best hope. He will tell her his story and ask if she is willing to make one more sacrifice. To be his champion too.

⟷⟷

As a student Gail has no peer. Learning the hobo signs is easy for her. Her mind already works in two strange languages: English and music. One more is welcome to join in. Soon Rembrandt begins to see things in her sign-work that are new to him. She isn't just learning the signs. She's improving, improvising on his years of trial and error.

He watches her as each hand makes separate signs, combining effects at a speed and with a flash that make his decades of practice look like chop-sticks.

Somehow in her tragedy, the fat has been pared away from her mind. Maybe this explains the obsessions, cleaning up broken glass and repeating numbers with machine-like precision. After the shooting, she'd been like an un-harnessed flywheel, running faster and faster, shaking itself to destruction.

She consumes his lessons more rapidly that he can speak. He is a 33 1/3 talking to a 78.

It's exhausting. He has to use skin-signs like *had a good sleep* and *full belly* just to keep going. Once, he pulls up his baggy trouser legs and adds *strength of a bear* and *alert and ready* to two skinny old shins.

Gail is beautiful. A woman untouchable.

After the first day Rembrandt watches over her as she sleeps through the night, undisturbed by dreams. Next morning, by silent consent they move camp to a new location, a quiet place in a city park. It seems necessary to make a fresh start.

On the second day they start the skin-signs and she never mentions going to watch the school. Counting the 3-5-9's has been banished from her thoughts.

Rembrandt feels real hope kindle in his heart. Eighty years of wandering. Losing Uncle Thompson. Pa's death. Leaving Ma and Three Farms. Leona. Those things had happened so long ago. But you can't grieve and move on when spirits still look to you for rescue. So those losses have been present with him every day since. The idea that he might at last have found *the* champion is a candle too bright to look at.

After the third day, Rembrandt starts covering the same ground. He has nothing left to teach her. It's Gail who says, "I'm ready."

Rembrandt puts Gail off to the fourth day, saying he wants to test her further, but they both know it's a sham. There isn't any sign that she can't do faster or better than him. So on the fourth day, Rembrandt tells her how to call the Devil. And she does.

46   Rembrandt — Paris, Kentucky — 1987

BACK IN 1987, when he was seventy, Rembrandt thought of himself as a wise old man. He'd seen a lot of the world and in the pretty little town of Paris, Kentucky believed that he had at last met "the one." As unlikely a champion as you could imagine Lisa was barely more than eighteen. The poor girl might have grown up fine but for a mother addicted to every kind of chemical the genius of man could imagine.

Born — never being wanted. Lived — never being loved.

Her first years of life spent going cold turkey to kick addictions she'd never chosen. But she had a spark that attracted him.

Ma had said, "Find someone who's lived a tough life." And he'd never seen tougher. What kind of pain could the Devil throw at this girl that she hadn't already overcome?

When Lisa called the Devil, she'd insisted on playing the overture from some space-opera movie. Said she'd use "The Force," whatever the hell that was.

After... after she failed, Rembrandt thought hard about killing himself.

The Black Bottle Man was there, to offer mock condolences and a leering smile.

"What have you done in your life that hasn't brought evil into the lives of others? You're the Devil's tool. A Siren calling broken little girls to risk any hope of joining the heavenly hosts, and for what?

"People they've never met and who mean nothing to them? The world would be a better place without you, old man. Come pay your penance in the fiery pit. You deserve it and more. All you have to do is stay down and when the thirteenth day comes I'll put an end to this farce."

But Uncle Thompson came to Rembrandt in a dream. In the dream his uncle, still a young man, now half his age, led him down the road west from Three Farms a piece and said, "Your pa will be along in a bit, and we'll catch some trout and have a feed."

So before sunset on the twelfth day he had been in a boxcar going... somewhere.

GAIL WANTS REMBRANDT'S ADVICE about where to fight the Black Bottle Man.

"Would a church be best? Or maybe a deserted cement factory?"

He can see that she is recovering a sense of humour that has been busy coping with the ironies of her own life. He holds onto a dead-pan expression and pretends to weigh the alternatives.

"Coffee shop," he suggests.

"A coffee shop? Any particular reason?"

"I haven't had breakfast yet," he says, "and I may need to take a leak."

There is no arguing with that, so a coffee shop it is. The waitress is a snippy little thing who seats them in a back booth next to the kitchen door. She gives the impression that she doesn't expect much of a tip out of these two and hands out a pair of plastic menus like Gail and Rembrandt can't be trusted with them.

"We're expecting another person to be joining us." Gail says. This elicits a fine display of eye rolling, but no third menu.

From her shoulder bag Gail extracts a gleaming green metal cylinder, bartered for yesterday at a swap-meet, purchased with her last remaining treasure. Come what may today, the tick of her prize metronome will not be heard tonight.

Gail stands the cylinder upright on the table, its domed top is split from the body by a thin line. It is a thermos, filled minutes before down the street with Rembrandt's favourite sacrament, Salvation Army morning coffee. Gail spins the lid, and a scent like kindness escapes into the room.

"No drinking that in here," the waitress says and Rembrandt thinks she must have practised her crosshatched expression in the mirror. It can't possibly be natural.

"Don't worry," Gail says. "I'm not planning to."

"Two coffees, please," Rembrandt intervenes, "and an order of rye toast, dry."

Cups are filled with a splash and the empress leaves. Rembrandt takes a sip and learns the secret origin of Her Majesty's hash-faced look.

Down through the years it has become evident to Rembrandt that Satan has his own sense of style. Not big and flashy like you might think; arriving at Three Farms with a rented team and rig was about as ordinary as things get.

No, the Black Bottle Man tries to blend in, like he could be anybody. Your neighbour. Your friend. It makes folks underestimate him. Remembering that, Rembrandt's confidence in Gail quavers.

Maybe it's the caffeine or the way a bell jangles when a family opens the coffee shop door to leave, but he feels jumpy. As the door swings shut again a boot stops it and a man in a black topcoat waves some giggling teenage girls in ahead of him.

Rembrandt can see a white rental van filling the handicapped parking spot near the front door. The Devil does like to have cargo space.

The man in black is not wearing his "glad-ta-meet-ya" smile. Rembrandt sincerely hopes that the man will not be happy to see them today.

Satan asks to join them and offers his hand to Gail. She declines.

"Another girl, Rembrandt?" the Black Bottle Man says. "What's our theme music this time? A selection from *The Lord of the Rings*?"

Ma would have liked Gail. No bravado. No warnings. She just gets straight to it.

She dips four fingers into the thermos of Sally Ann coffee, swipes Billy's doubled thunderbolt skin-sign for *lightning speed*, first on her arm, and then on Rembrandt's, and flings the entire remaining contents of the thermos up into the air. The steaming liquid spreads like a black-lace curtain between Gail and the Black Bottle Man, slowing as it rises.

Then Gail flickers — left hand, right hand. Both hands moving in the air, hummingbird quick, making hobo signs on the table and in the air, flicking drops of coffee on her arms to make skin-signs that shine like black pearls.

There are symbols Rembrandt knows well, right from the earliest days sitting with the hobo gentlemen, learning along with Pa and Uncle Thompson. They are linked and married to signs it has taken him years to create. And then new signs!

Ones she must have dreamt up in her head, like inside-out musical notes. One looks like the numerals 3-5-9 repeating off into infinity.

But none of the signs are doing anything to the Black Bottle Man. Because she isn't attacking him. No. She's building a structure of signs, like a pyramid of power.

Rembrandt remembers the dimpled clay tablet in Professor Ginsberg's study and suddenly understands her intent. Like the letters of a word or the notes of a musical phrase, each hobo sign has its own purpose, but he'd never found a way to make them work together, to meld them into something greater: like a story or a composition.

Alone, what emotion can a single note convey? What power can one letter command?

But weave them together and they can become the words to a story, or the movements of a symphony, able to inspire the hearts of nations.

As her creation grows Rembrandt sees that when Gail completes the pyramid, if she can complete it, then all the signs, everything he has learned and gathered and created in eighty years of wandering, plus all that she's found in that guilt-crazy head of hers will coalesce, not into music, not into a story, but into a single, perfect word.

Like a word from the lips of God.

The Devil just sits there, waiting. He isn't fighting back or even trying to unmake Gail's creation. He just watches her. It's like...he recognizes what she is creating; like he wants to hear that word. Like he's been waiting all the ages since The Fall to hear God speak again.

Rembrandt wonders, who is the Devil? What would it be like to be him? To converse at the right hand of God and then to be cast down? To never hear the true word of the Lord again? What would he want?

That kind of Devil wouldn't care about scraping up a few more souls. Souls aren't so precious. People sell their salvation every day for a bit of extra attention.

Then Gail's beautiful creation is complete and the Black Bottle Man murmurs something Rembrandt would never have expected to hear the Fallen Angel say.

"In the beginning was The Word."

The curtain of coffee is gone and the pyramid is capped and ready. One final touch and it will collapse all the prayers that Rembrandt has ever heard or said, and God will speak.

And...the Devil will have what he wants. What he's pushed Rembrandt and his family toward all these years. What he's shaped Rembrandt to do, to give birth to.

A new Beginning.

A new Creation.

A second chance to overthrow God.

And the souls of the aunts and Pa and Uncle Thompson, the souls of Uncle Billy and all the other proud champions who'd tried to beat the Devil — and the soul pledged by a brave ten-year-old boy, will still belong to the Black Bottle Man.

Rembrandt reaches out and takes Gail's hand, as gentle as the Lamb.

"Wait," he says, and looks across the table, across a gulf of pain and loss at the Black Bottle Man.

"Concede," he says. He feels his pa's hand on his shoulder, like that last day in the new clap-board church. "Give up. You're beat."

Gail looks at him, a line notches her brow.

"It's okay," he tells her. "You've done it. You've beat the Devil. You see? Don't give the Devil what he wants, and you've beat him."

The Black Bottle Man doesn't disagree. He looks longingly at Gail's creation and starts to speak. "I, I can offer you—"

But Gail doesn't wait to hear the rest. She holds out her hand and the pyramid dwindles, and shrinks, and disappears with a *pop*.

"Let God speak for himself, if he has a mind to."

⚜

Souls are sent on to Jesus, the rye toast arrives and the Devil departs.

The way his rental van leaves that parking lot, the Black Bottle Man might not be getting his damage deposit back.

Rembrandt excuses himself to use the Men's. "At my age, coffee goes right to my bladder."

In the privacy of the restroom he splashes cold water on his face and gives thanks to God...along with a piece of his mind.

Sitting down in the booth again he sees a slice of his toast is gone. Gail is taking a big bite out of it.

"Sorry," she shrugs. "I gave in to temptation."

ON SUNDAY MORNING Ray stops by Gail's cardboard nest to leave a bowl of porridge. But she isn't there. And she isn't at the school on Monday, so he files a missing person's report.

Walking home he passes St. Michael's Church, where in happier times he and Gail had been married. It's a somber limestone building, serious about God's business. But the noise coming from the open front doors doesn't sound serious. People are...laughing?

From the doorway he sees her.

Gail.

She's smiling and joking with the priests and nuns. It's like they draw solace from her, just as he once had.

She looks up. Sees him. Recognizes him. And does not run.

49 Rembrandt — 2007

FROM A PEW AT THE BACK of the church Rembrandt watches Gail and Raymond, reunited.

He and Gail had come to St. Michael's on Gail's account. Since the shooting she hadn't been to confession and felt it was about time.

Rembrandt was all set to hear the kind of fire and brimstone sermon his presence usually evoked, but this time it didn't happen. Something had changed and it didn't take long to figure out what. All those years, those ministers and priests, they'd been right to chastise him. He *had* been on the Devil's errand. But now that's done.

From a pocket he extracts a carefully folded packet he's been carrying these past few days. Gail's unsent letter. He places it in her hands, returning all the secrets she had entrusted to him the night they'd met on her concrete stairwell.

Words on paper have a healing magic of their own and he hopes the letter might help Raymond and Gail rebuild the miracle of marriage.

The little lake is still beautiful. Green farms are still cupped by tall mountains. No steam rises from the sugar beet plant, closed in 1967.

Rembrandt feels as nervous as a bridegroom, climbing down the Greyhound's steps onto the main street of Sugar City, Colorado.

Ninety years plus thirty-one days have passed. And he is still living.

That was another of the Devil's lies. It isn't Satan who gives life.

It's family. And love.

He has walked this mountain road a hundred times before, to see Leona. He will walk it one more time. Home at last.

Acknowledgments

My thanks:

To my mother, Lillian Russell, who raised ten children on a Manitoba dirt farm with unmatched grace. *A kind woman lives here.*

To the original true friend hobos - Mike MacFarlane, Paul St. Pierre, Shen Braun and Alex Braun – who were there at the beginning.

To drama instructor, Nancy Drake, for teaching me to think like an actor.

To rough-draft-readers, Margaret Pople, James Warnez, Roger Rigelhof and Marjorie Russell, for your early reassurances.

To Lisa Vasconcelos and the Mecca Productions actors who brought this story to life on stage in Brandon, Manitoba in 2008 — Brett Bews, Emilie Blaikie, Bill Bolley, Shen Braun, Klaus Brechmann, Bob Brereton, Bailey Forester, Mike Forester, Ken Jackson, Brenda Lacerte, Brent Legg, Colleen Moman, Tiffany Muckle, Avery Penner, Christine Penner, Shirley Pogson, Marilyn Ross, Marie Russell-Yearwood, Paul St. Pierre and James Warnez. For me, these characters will always speak with your voices.

To Rory Runnells of the Manitoba Association of Playwrights, playwright Bruce McManus and Manitoba Theatre Centre producer Laurie Lam, the professionals who lent me their confidence.

To David Bergen, who, as a guest instructor at C.M.U., asked for a closer examination of "one moonless summer night" and inspired chapter four.

To Kristine Dmytrak, designer at Relish Designs, for a great book cover.

To Anita Daher, editor at Great Plains Publications. No author could ask for a more ardent supporter or insightful editor.

To Gregg Shilliday and Catharina de Bakker at Great Plains Publications, for your attention to detail and commitment to excellence.

To Peter Jackson, who I really, really wish would direct the film version of this book.

And most of all to my wife Janet, my best friend.

The hymn quoted in Chapter Forty-Two is *Blessed Be The Tie That Binds*, written by John Fawcett (1740-1817).

The song quoted in Chapter 30 is *Mairzy Doats*, written by Milton Drake, Al Hoffman and Jerry Livingston.

The Sumerian text in Chapter 43 is paraphrased from a translation of *Lugalbanda and the Anzu Bird* written by J.A. Black, G. Cunningham, E. Robson and G. Zlyomi.